*Pra*y ... ...

...ombe

a novelette
by

Belinda Roberts

based on the relations
of the lovers originally created
by Jane Austen
in her cracking bestseller,
'Pride and Prejudice'

To my delightful family at Longbourn

Prawn and Prejudice was first published
in the United Kingdom in 2009
as an original paperback by Beetleheart Publishing.

ISBN 978 0 9540208 5 9

belinda.roberts@beetleheart.co.uk
www.beetleheart.co.uk

Chapter One

IT is a truth universally acknowledged, that a single man in possession of a yacht must be in want of a female crew.

It was this that occupied the mind of Mrs Bennet as she stepped purposefully out from her holiday house at 3 Island Street, Salcombe, strode along Victoria Quay and up Fore Street, drawn hypnotically towards the divinely glamorous world of Amelia's Attic, with only the vaguest notion of what she would do there when she arrived, apart from browse a little and browse a little more. It just seemed a perfectly respectable place to be heading and it was so important to look busy and wanted. As she passed The Upper Crust Bakery delicious warming aromas caused her to pause, but one look at the queue of Crew clad shoppers dangling jute bags as proof of their environmentally friendly lifestyle in one hand and jangling their 4 x 4 keys in deep pockets with the other, made her swerve to the right side of the narrow street. She was just considering the fudge in Cranch's when a squawk made her swivel her head violently to port.

'Yahoo! Frances! Darling! Have you heard the news?'

It was Mrs Lucas, flushed with excitement.

Kiss. Kiss. Kiss.

'Of course, darling.' Mrs Bennet never liked to appear not in the know. 'What on earth is it?'

'Look. Are you busy? Never mind if you are. Come with me to The Wardroom for a cappuccino and I'll tell you what the whole of Salcombe society is talking about!'

Mrs Bennet found herself being scooped up Fore Street, arm in arm with her best friend, Mrs Lucas, and over a cup of steaming cappuccino being the recipient of startling and delightful news.

'A man of great fortune is said to have taken Netherpollock!'

Netherpollock! A magnificent seaside villa with large bay windows situated on the opposite side of the estuary, perched just above Small's Cove with fabulous views of the harbour's comings and goings. How splendid.

'... and what's more,' continued Mrs Lucas, breathless,

'... he is young ...'

Young!

'... and single!'

Single!

This was too much. Mrs Bennet spluttered on her cappuccino sending a frothy spray over her unfortunate friend. This *was* news indeed! Gulping down her refreshment with the utmost speed, not even pausing to use her teaspoon to scrape any residual froth from the bottom of the cup as was her normal custom, Mrs Bennet muttered something about having to catch the post - her usual excuse although how rare it was these days to put pen to paper - and dashed off back to Island Street.

'News, Mr Bennet! News!'

Mr Bennet, happy to be on holiday in Island Street with its lively mix of activity - boatyards, chandlers, art galleries, tanks of live crabs and lobsters, the sounds of craftsmen banging, chipping and sawing - was still in his striped pyjamas peacefully reading The Daily Telegraph in the little flagstone kitchen of No 3. Spurning the plate of foreign croissants, he was enjoying a hearty piece of thick toast spread with thick butter and thick marmalade, when the explosive high pitched sounds pierced his ears from two streets away. An installment of his wife's 'news' was hard to bear. A sale on at Jack Wills? A new diamante bag in Amelia's Attic? He closed his eyes, savouring the last moments of sanity.

The front door slammed open and the front door slammed shut. Heavy breathing and six hurried footsteps down the wooden planked hall followed and Mrs Bennet burst into the kitchen.

'Mr Bennet! Oh Mr Bennet! Have you heard? Netherpollock is let at last!'

Mr Bennet opened his eyes, adjusted his specs and read that 20% of married men confess to having considered leaving their wives at least once. 'Only 20%!' he muttered.

'20%? No the whole lot!' retorted Mrs Bennet. 'A young man of large fortune from the north of England has taken it.'

Mrs Bennet paused, reflecting on her own words. North was not as promising as south but she was prepared to remain open minded.

'And is his wife charming and dressed from head to toe in Joules clothing?'

'His *wife*? Oh Mr Bennet! How you tease me! He is single to be sure! *Young* and single! Is that not a fine thing for our girls!'

'How so? How can it affect them?'

'My dear Mr Bennet! How can you be so tiresome? You must know that I am thinking of him going out with one of them and if we are lucky marrying one of them.'

'Is that his design in taking Netherpollock?'

'Design? Nonsense! How can you talk so! But it is very likely that he may fall in love with one of them and therefore you must go up to the Yacht Club for a drink this lunchtime for he is sure to be there and make his acquaintance'

'Why don't you go and take the girls with you? Then he can see which he prefers and who knows - he might even choose you!'

'Oh Mr Bennet. You know I cannot go on my own or with the girls. It would look too obvious. Too pushy! No. You must go and fall into friendly conversation with him. Talk about tax cuts, budgets, financially sort of things. Make his acquaintance.'

'You go and I will send a note along with you saying he can marry whichever of my daughters he chooses, though I must throw in a good word for my little Lizzy!'

'Oh Mr Bennet! It's always Lizzy, Lizzy, Lizzy. She is no

better than the others. Yet you always favour her!'

'They have none of them much to recommend them; minds stuffed with fashion, ears stuffed with ipod intrusions, mouths stuffed with chupa chups. No ability for normal conversation or comment on the world,' replied Mr Bennet. 'They are gormless and half-witted like most of their generation; but Lizzy shows the occasional spark of being able to function like a reasonable human being.'

'Mr Bennet! These are *our* girls you are ridiculing. Our babies. Oh! Oh! You have dehydrated me with your venomous talk. Oh! I am all palpitations. I need to detox. I need purified water. Oh lord! My stress levels are rising. I can feel them! Can you see them Mr Bennet? Can you see them?'

Mr Bennet looked at his wife and shook his head.

'Oh Mr Bennet, you have never cared for my stress levels.'

Mrs Bennet sat down heavily, holding her heaving chest, gasping for breath.

'You mistake me, my dear. I have a high respect for your levels. They are the barometer of my life. I have been party to their rises and falls for the past fifteen years.'

'Oh Mr Bennet. You take delight in vexing me. You have no compassion for my nerves either.'

'No!' interrupted Mr Bennet with severity and raising his hand to halt further comment. 'Not your nerves! *They* are my old friends whom I have heard you mention with consideration these *twenty* years at least and I will not have *them* dragged into this conversation too.'

'Ah! you do not know what I suffer,' cried the panting Mrs Bennet.

Mr Bennet returned to his calm, reasonable manner adding, 'But I am sure your attack will soon pass and you will recover to see Salcombe soon overflowing with young men of good fortune and our girls will have the courage to speak with them direct.'

There was a clanking on the wooden stairs. Lydia, the youngest Miss Bennet, dressed in buttock revealing pink spotted pants and a lacy singlet top shuffled into the kitchen, robotically put on the kettle, fumbled in the cupboard for a mug, blobbed in a teaspoon of Nescafé, slumped down onto one of the six pastel blue kitchen chairs and yawned vigorously. Her presence created a pause between Mr and Mrs Bennet. Mrs Bennet had temporarily run out of steam, unable to maintain continuing signs of dangerous stress and after a formal 'Good morning Lydia' to his daughter from which he expected and obtained, no response, Mr Bennet returned to his paper.

Chapter Two

AT lunchtime Mr Bennet did indeed venture to the Yacht Club and there, just as Mrs Bennet had predicted was the young man in question sitting in the window, having a quiet gin and tonic whilst earnestly tapping away on his laptop. Mr Bennet introduced himself as Mr Bennet and the young man leapt to his feet and shook hands.

'Delighted to meet you Mr Bonnet.'

'Bennet'

'No I'm Bingley. Mr Bingley.'

'And I'm Mr Bennet.'

'Who then sir,' asked the beaming Mr Bingley, 'is Mr Bonnet? I am new around here and not familiar with the names.'

'There is no Mr Bonnet.'

'How strange! I'm sure you mentioned him earlier. Perhaps he is a shy fellow but I would be pleased to meet him as I have few acquaintances in Salcombe. But what a splendid place it is is it not Mr Bonnet!'

'Bennet.'

'Oh Bennet! Bonnet! Such similar names. It must cause you quite a confusion.'

Mr Bennet found the young man in question most amiable, and discovered that his new acquaintance had quite a unique and captivating understanding of the world. On the effect of a credit crunch the young fellow enthused that as far as he understood, it was a fabulously healthy cereal, that employing hedge fund managers was the only way to keep the rabbits out of one's vegetable garden and from what he had seen so far in Salcombe, the bottom line seemed jolly attractive. Mr Bennet was rarely so entertained and invited Mr Bingley round to a barbeque that very evening, an invitation which the young man, having no acquaintances in the vicinity, accepted with alacrity.

The hot summer's day, meanwhile had passed in the usual Salcombe manner for Mrs Bennet and her five daughters. After breakfast the girls had set out for town, armed with regulation jute bags to gather supplies for a picnic. Lizzy and Jane had queued at The Upper Crust for six deliciously soft dough rolls sprinkled with sunflower seeds, whilst Lydia and Kitty had gone round to the deli to buy slices of ham and little quiche pies. The younger girls were seriously delayed by a detour into Cranch's, the sweetie shop where they spent a good fifteen minutes holding little plastic baskets and selecting fizzy coke cola chews, luminous green snakes, rainbow crystals and pink shrimps with plastic tongs before exiting, clutching pink and white stripped paper bags of goodies. Mary meanwhile remained back at 3 Island Street in the front room where passers by could peer in and see her swotting for her AS exams. She perched her physics textbook in the window so people could see that she was a girl of intellectual substance not one to be drawn into softy subjects like media studies - the very thought! The baffled frown on her face showed the intense challenge that such a mission as physics could present even to the brightest student.

The picnic at last prepared and packed into outsize waterproof bags printed with strawberry patterns, the little party was ready to venture out to the beach.

Beaches at Salcombe are either a little distance from the centre of town, North and South Sands or across the estuary - or dendritic ria as Mary had once discovered and enjoyed correcting anyone ignorant enough get the distinction wrong - lie the glorious ribbons of golden sands known as Fisherman's Cove, Small's Cove, Mill Bay, Sunny Cove, and for those with boats, The Bar.

Visitors delight in the fun of the ferries to get about from the town to the beaches or even up to Kingsbridge. The sturdy Salcombe to South Sands ferry ploughing back and forth, with its gaily fluttering flags and packed with holiday makers waving buckets and spades, who have the added pleasure of disembarking onto a fine sea tractor to ensure a dry landing on the beach, is a regular sight. Many locals and holiday house owners, however, have invested in some sort of craft to take them from beach to beach at their leisure. So it was a pleasant hundred foot walk to the wooden jetty where 'Angelica', a 12' grey inflatable, dearly loved by the Bennet family, was patiently waiting, that the girls and Mrs Bennet headed, laden with one large wicker picnic basket, three Cath Kidston patterned picnic bags, buckets, spades, cricket kit, rugby ball, tennis ball, towels, swimming gear, handbags, books, magazines, newspapers, windbreakers and lifejackets. Mrs Bennet liked to think of herself as 'good in boats'. Her inability to start the 6hp engine, distinguish a bowline from a clove hitch or cast off did not deter her from barking instructions. Transferring her weight from the pontoon and down into the bouncy boat always caused Angelica to lurch alarmingly and cause a slight heart flutter in Mrs Bennet's bosom but she was game and shouted and bossed the girls around so efficiently that she had a hand to help her from the pontoon, a hand to catch her into the boat, a hand to steady her posterior onto the thwart and a hand to pass her the overflowing and very unseaworthy handbag that followed her everywhere.

Lizzy pulled at the engine and after two attempts it chuckled into life. 'Cast off! Cast off!' shouted Mrs Bennet imperiously. 'Oh look! There are the Lucas's in 'Fly-by-night' Yahoo! Yahoo! I say Marcia, yahoo! Wave girls! Wave!'

The Lucas family were sailing by in their splendid Salcombe Yawl, a traditional wooden boat with two masts - main and mizzen - much beloved by Salcombe society.

'Oh I say! Frances! Yahoo!' echoed Mrs Lucas, spotting the overloaded Angelica. 'Wonderful news! Charlotte's 'A' level results!'

'What did you say?' cried Mrs Bennet across the water, and standing up as if she could get a little closer by doing so. 'Go over to Fly-by-night Lizzy! I can't hear what Marcia is saying.'

'She's like, trying to tell you how brilliantly Charlotte has done in her 'A' levels,' interjected Kitty mischievously.

As best friends Mrs Bennet would naturally want to share in Marcia's happiness. But *her* girls were expecting results too. It could be awkward.

'Sorry Marcia! Can't hear you. Catch up later!' shouted Mrs Bennet, adding the command, 'Head for the beach Lizzy!' to which Lizzy responded with such alacrity that Mrs Bennet, caught off balance, was pitched head first across the bows, her legs shooting up into the air in a most unladylike fashion and her handbag flung skyward. The girls could not help but dissolve into peals of laughter, fortunately catching the airborne bag, saving it from a watery grave. The whole incident would have been forgotten if it had not been splendidly caught on camera by a passing professional photographer in a speedboat who specialised in capturing those magical family moments. Later that day Mr Bennet recognising his wife's legs, her handbag and his merry daughters on display in a picture in the photographer's shop window was so taken by the artistic merit of the shot that he ordered a large print immediately which gave him much cause to chuckle for many years to come.

Mrs Bennet and handbag now recovered, the party continued on their voyage across the estuary, dodging lasers, toppers and luxury cruisers reaching Mill Bay without any further adventure, where Lizzy skillfully drove the boat to shallow water and Lydia and Kitty leapt out in bare feet, screeching and laughing partly at the coldness of the water and partly for the benefit of some fit young men in Jack Wills' pants. Within five minutes the little party had joined another fifty or so families on the beach, shielded by colourful windshields, with picnics at the ready, books to read, the sparkling sea before them and nothing much more to do than chill out. Bliss.

As they settled down on multi-coloured beach towels to read, or in Lydia and Kitty's case, to gossip, Mr Bennet clad in his customary long navy shorts, pale blue shirt and panama hat appeared, unnoticed and stood behind the windshield gazing at the hectic scenes of boating antics before him.

'Oh if only Mr Bennet would go and visit Mr Bingley! Marcia is bound to connive to snatch the young man for one of *her* daughters. I am sure of it!'

The outburst came from Mrs Bennet who had been lying on the beach fretting over the day's events.

'If you are so sure it is a shame I have wasted my time chatting to Mr Bingley,' said Mr Bennet. The sound of his voice with no sense of his body caused Mrs Bennet to shriek in alarm. 'Mr Bennet!'

Catching sight of him over the windshield and assured it was not a ghost she proceeded, most anxiously to quiz him.

'What do you mean you have been chatting with Mr Bingley?'

'I mean I have been chatting to Mr Bingley. A delightful young man who will be joining us for a barbeque this evening!'

This was too much for Mrs Bennet to take in all at once! Joy overwhelmed her and words for once failed her. Instead she leapt up and to the delight of the beach, and, as one onlooker said, 'gave the poor chap a right smacker!'

Chapter Three

MRS BENNET and the girls spent the morning discussing what the barbeque would consist of only to be quashed in their enthusiasm by a message received on Mr Bennet's phone from young Mr Bingley informing them he had made a diary error and would in fact be in Dartmouth that evening and be unable to join them. Mrs Bennet was most vexed and commented that she hoped he was not going to be one of those young men who was constantly flitting from one thing to another and could never be trusted to make up his mind. Her anxieties, however, were assuaged when Mr Bennet read out the remainder of the message.

'Soz Mr Bonnet but will be back 2 Salcombe 2morrow with friends on 62ft yacht 'Pemberley'. All invited for drinks. Bingley.'

'A sixty-two foot yacht! He must be a *very* wealthy young man!' exclaimed Mrs Bennet in delight, quite forgetting her anxiety about his flightiness.

Discussion now transferred from the barbeque to what one should wear for drinks at noon on a sixty-two foot yacht.

'I shall wear like my new pink sundress from Fat Face,' declared Kitty. 'Although I have only worn it like once, I have seen many a young man turn their heads to stare at me.'

'In horror,' concluded Lydia.

'Beast,' retorted Kitty tearfully. 'Mother tell Lydia not to be so mean.'

'I think you look most fetching in pink Kitty dear,' said Mrs Bennet, 'and Lydia you must wear your yellow satin with the little matching bandanna.'

'Yellow mother? Joke on!' retorted Lydia. 'No I will wear

Kitty's pink. I look so much more glamourous in it than she does!'

'What! Have you, like, dared to try it on?' Kitty sat up in horror.

'Only once – and it suited me perfectly.'

'Really. How childish you girls are,' interjected Mary. 'I for one will not be taking up such an invitation. I have my physics and my future to consider.'

'Whateva,' snorted Lydia and the conversation continued in such a vein for some time. The eldest two Bennet girls took the opportunity to slip away and enjoy a deep meaningful conversation while strolling along the beach.

'How Lydia and Kitty go on,' laughed Jane.

'They drive me to distraction,' replied Lizzy, picking up a smooth, flat pebble and skimming it across the calm sea. 'But you Jane, why, you have the patience of an angel.'

Jane smiled, unable to think of a response. Lizzy continued teasingly. 'But even angels may wish to fall in love and marry, Jane. Have you considered what you will wear tomorrow for you are surely the prettiest of us all and by far the sweetest natured and have the most chance of landing a prize catch.'

'Oh Lizzy. How you tease me. I have given it very little thought, but now you come to mention it I think I will wear my pale blue.'

Jane laughed and the girls, reaching the end of the beach, scrambled over the rocks to consider the matter further whilst poking around in the rock pools.

In the event Mr Bennet was diverted by business matters and was unable to join the party venturing out to drinks on Pemberley so the girls (including Mary who persuaded herself that a few hours in constructive leisure may refresh her mind and therefore be beneficial to her studies) went only accompanied by their mother. Mrs Bennet was vexed that Lydia had insisted on dressing in her seriously short shorts but apart from this was in good spirits as they left the safety of the shore and travelled over the estuary waters in Angelica to where they understood Pemberley to be at anchor. Unfortunately Mrs Bennet had misunderstood Mr Bennet's directions and by the time they had putt-putted up the inlets to Southpool, then Frogmore and practically all the way to Kingsbridge with no sign of the magnificent Pemberley Mrs Bennet was becoming agitated.

'Oh lord! We are so late! It will be tea-time before we arrive. We will make such a terrible impression!' At that moment Lizzy's mobile rang. It was Charlotte Lucas.

'Oh Lizzy! Thank-goodness you have answered. Listen I am at a drinks party on a yacht and have just overheard the delightful Mr Bingley saying how disappointed he is that your family is not here. He has heard much of your reputation as hotties and was looking forward to judging for himself! Are you not coming?'

'Hotties!' Lizzy laughed. 'Yes Charlotte – we are intending to come directly but I fear we are lost – or at least Pemberley is lost to us!'

'What?' interjected Mrs Bennet. 'Is Charlotte Lucas already on board? Trust Marcia to think only of her *own* daughter! Find out where the yacht is. Hurry Lizzy! Hurry!'

'Mother, please! The line is poor enough. I can barely hear dear Charlotte.'

In time Lizzy managed to hush Mrs Bennet, ascertain the location of the yacht and instruct Lydia, who was at Angelica's helm, to head in the right direction.

There was much shrieking and wobbling of the boat as the girls disembarked from Angelica and climbed the wooden step ladder to board Pemberley. And what a splendid yacht it was indeed. sixty-two foot long – or an inch or so more – with fine varnished decks, polished brass instruments, two masts that seemed to touch the sky, furled round with the whitest of sails All this was enough to take one's breath away, but wha captivated the girls most - and Mrs Bennet the very most -

was Mr Bingley. Mr Bingley was good looking and gentlemanlike; he had a pleasant countenance, and easy, unaffected manners. He seemed equally captivated, waving away the Bennet's apologies for being late, and helping each one on board with delight. One could not help but notice his sharp intake of breath on first beholding Jane and how he took a little longer helping *her* on board, and how his eye's followed her every move and how attentive he was to her every possible requirement for a drink, or perhaps a little shade, or to ensure she did suffer from too strong a breeze, or was not made giddy by the gentle rocking of the boat.

Champagne was served and all was jollity and delight. Mr Bingley introduced his visitors to his sisters Cazza, Lulu and Hattie, who attempted civility before taking out their towels, lying down towards the bows, closing their eyes and busying themselves with sunbathing. Mrs Bennet, so put out initially to find Mrs Lucas already on board, soon fell into discussion with her dear friend and both agreed that Mr Bingley was the perfect young man.

'To think,' whispered Mrs Bennet, 'that such a young man should own not only Netherpollock but also such a fine yacht.'

'Oh Mrs Bennet! You are mistaken. Mr Bingley may own Netherpollock but he does not own this yacht. No. That honour goes to his good friend Mr Darcy!'

'Mr Darcy! And who is he?' asked Mrs Bennet most puzzled.

At that very moment Mr Bingley seemed to come out of his entrancement with Jane and called in a loud voice 'I say Darcy! Do come and join us! We have guests! Darcy!'

All eyes looked to the front of the yacht where stood a tall, dark figure no-one had previously observed. Now hearing his name, the gentleman in question turned and immediately drew gasps of admiration from all the ladies, thrilled by his fine, tall person, his impressive physic set off perfectly by a fabulously British blue and white striped cotton shirt with sleeves rolled up to reveal strong, muscular arms, dark blue shorts revealing strong, muscular legs, handsome features, noble mien and the fact that circulated almost immediately that his fortune was tenfold that of Mr Bingley's.

'Oh Lord!' exclaimed Mrs Bennet, in an excited whisper on receiving this news. 'He is far handsomer than Mr Bingley. He would make the better husband!'

Bingley clambered forward over the deck to speak with urgency to Darcy.

'Come Darcy. I must have you join our guests. I hate to see you standing about by yourself in this stupid manner. You had much better join us.'

'I certainly shall not. There is no woman aboard who I would wish to waste my time with. And you are talking to the only handsome girl.'

'Oh she is the hottest tottie I every beheld! But there is one of her sisters sitting down just behind you, who is very pretty, and I dare say, splendidly agreeable. Do let me introduce you.'

'Which do you mean?'

Turning round Darcy looked for a moment at Lizzy who was perched on the cabin roof, and catching her eye momentarily withdrew his own.

'Boo that! She is tolerable; but not handsome enough to tempt me. You had better return to your partner and enjoy her smiles, for you are wasting your time with me.'

With that Darcy turned away and continued his brooding stare out over the estuary. Bingley, perplexed by his friend's stupid behaviour, clambered back over the deck to further enjoy the company of those in the cockpit. Lizzy, who had overheard Mr Darcy's remark, felt he was indeed a proud and unpleasant man, so was not hurt and enjoyed regaling the story to her friends.

The drinks party drew to a close, and the Bennet party returned without further incident to 3 Island Street where the rest of the day was spent recounting the events aboard Pemberley. Mr Bennet was told if not once, but a thousand times, by Mrs Bennet, how delightful Mr Bingley was, how h admired Jane and how he favoured her above all others and only when Mr Bennet protested that he had heard enough did Mrs Bennet look for another avenue for her story and recounted the shocking rudeness of Mr Darcy. 'He is the most disagreeable, horrid man, so high and so conceited that there was no enduring him! I quite detest the man!' And with that Mrs Bennet flounced out of the room and Mr Bennet was left once more, grateful for silence and solitude.

Chapter Four

'OH Lizzy' cried Jane 'I must confess, he is a blaze! The most delightful, handsomest, cutest guy I have ever had the good fortune to set eyes on.'

'And you Jane are quite the most delightful, handsomest, cutest girl *he* has ever had the good fortune to set eyes on. The perfect match.'

'Oh don't tease me Lizzy. And what of his sisters? Were they not awesome? Quite the most elegant creatures you ever beheld?'

'Elegant they may be but proud and unfriendly. First they spent their time frazzling in the sun to avoid conversation with us and when this became too dull for them they talked only to themselves, constantly keeping to starboard when we were on port and when we moved to port I could not fail to notice that they moved straight away to starboard.'

'Oh Lizzy! I am sure they meant nothing of that. They were simply trying to keep the boat well balanced for our comfort.'

Lizzy was not convinced but did not pursue the matter for fear of upsetting Jane. Bingley's sisters were indeed fashionable ladies, educated at a reassuringly expensive public school, who had inherited a fortune healthy enough to keep them active in the clothes shops around Sloane Square when in London – a hobby that for the summer season was being successfully maintained by diligent visits to the clothes shops of Salcombe. Along with regular visits to the birthplace of Jack Wills, Crew, Joules, Fat Face, White Stuff, Quba Sails and Amelia's Attic had all felt the beneficence of the young ladies and had happily yielded up their designer carrier bags to allow jackets, hats, stripy shirts, polos, hoodies, sweatpants and jewellery to be transported back to Netherpollock.

Mr Bingley himself had inherited an equally fine amount of money on the passing away of his father. This had been a most distressing time since Bingley was only a young fellow with his life ahead of him and barely out of 'A' levels. His intention to spend it on bricks and mortar had been encouraged by his older sisters who planned to escape the north and spend *their* inheritance on houses in London but were keen to encourage *him* to buy a holiday house in Devon where they could all holiday and keep the family together in such sorry times. The sisters contacted agents in Devon and Cornwall and soon tempting residences were dropping through the letterbox. But Bingley, still in mourning for his father, and with the likelihood of re-takes looming was proving obstinately slow at doing anything with his new found wealth. It was only on a visit to the dentist that Lulu, reading a surprisingly up-to-date copy of 'Country Life' saw 'a gem of the Devon coastline' for sale, immediately fell in love with it on behalf of Chas, popped the magazine in her Gucci bag and within half an hour of leaving the dentist with a numb jaw had left the magazine open on the kitchen table of their family home in the north. And so it was that the young Bingley spotted Netherpollock in Country Life, announced to his sisters that 'Dash it all! It's what the parentals would have wanted', and that he must have it, caught a train to Devon, a taxi straight to Salcombe, a water taxi across to Netherpollock where he met the affable agent, ran around the house enthusing at its splendid views, its delightful proportions and was generally so happy and satisfied with everything that he

18

put an offer in there and then and did not sleep soundly until he had exchanged and the property was his.

Happy in Netherpollock, happy with his sisters, happy with his steady friendship with Darcy, Bingley could not have been more different from the latter. Whereas Bingley was all smiles, Darcy was all grumps; Bingley made friends wherever he went, Darcy always managed to offend. But Bingley admired Darcy and took note of his judgement – Darcy after all was superior in intellect, not that Bingley was totally deficient. It was a reflection of his easy going nature that Bingley was not offended by Darcy's superior, fastidious nature and the two spent much time in each other's company. The manner in which they discussed the Pemberley drinks party perfectly reflected their characters. Bingley enthused he had never met such splendidly, delightful girls in his life, whereas Darcy complained he had never seen a collection of people for whom he had so little regard. He did admit that the eldest Miss Bennet was very pretty, but she smiled too much.

On the subject of Jane Bennet the Bingley sisters agreed that she was a pretty, sweet girl whom they could tolerate in company. This was enough encouragement for Bingley to feel he could think of her as he chose.

Chapter Five

OPPOSITE 3 Island Street, where the Bennet family resided during their summer holidays was Island Terrace where the Lucas family resided during their summer holidays. Sir William Lucas had worked in his family business, a shop entitled 'Knitter's Paradise' as a young man, and had enjoyed a steady income for minimal effort for many years allowing him to be tempted into standing as a local councillor, which, upon election he devoted himself to his duties with surprising vigour and with unparalled enthusiasm for health and safety issues. So much so that he had managed to close down many dangerous businesses in his local town as well as the scouts, rugby club, Sunday school, art class and pilates for the over 80's, saving lives and limbs, and ultimately resulting in his presentation at St James's for service to the community. But Sir William had paid a price for his diligence. The little town, now safe, was devoid of hustle and bustle. In short it had become so stiflingly dull that Sir William was forced to move out during the summer months for there was nothing for his children to do. He had cast around for a place to buy a holiday house, and being a man with a nose for fashion realised one could not go wrong with Salcombe and also being a man of inherited means had enough money to be generous without causing himself too much distress. So it was with a warm heart he arrived in Salcombe ready to sprinkle health and safety advice on locals and fellow holiday makers.

His wife Marcia was a talented chatterbox, but not too clever not to be a valuable neighbour to Mrs Bennet. They had several children, the eldest of which Charlotte, a sensible, intelligent young woman was Lizzy's intimate friend.

An event like drinks on the Pemberley could not go undiscussed by the Lucas and Bennet families and so it was not surprising to see a group of them sitting on the jetty, enjoying ice-creams and conversing over the previous day's events.

'You were favoured with early conversation with Mr Bingley, my dear Lottie,' said Mrs Bennet generously.

'Oh yes! We had a most interesting discussion about university. To think a young man should have a house in Salcombe and at the same time be applying to university. Why! It is most uncommon!'

'I doubt he will take out a loan.'

'A loan! Heaven's child! A man of Mr Bingley's means would not need such a thing as a loan. He has all the money in the world! A loan indeed!'

'University? Why I doubt he will be going anyway now he has gone completely loopy over Jane!' said Kitty.

'Really Kitty!' interjected Mary. 'How could you speak in such ignorant terms. A young man of intelligence will always choose education over romance.'

'Oh chill out Mary!'

'Why should I! My opinions are just as valuable as anyone else's. In fact, I would go further to say that in the present company they are probably *more* valuable.'

Mary licked her pistachio ice-cream with vigour to prove her point.

'And what about Mr Darcy? Wasn't he insanely rude to poor Lizzy!'

'He is very proud,' said Lizzy smiling. 'But I suppose he is a fine young man, rich and with everything he could wish for so I suppose you could forgive him for being a little proud. In fact, I could easily forgive his pride, if he hadn't mortified mine.'

Chapter Six

As the summer days slipped by the Bennets saw more and more of the Bingley party. Angelica proved invaluable for popping backwards and forwards to Netherpollock and Mill Bay. Bingley soon purchased his own rib, which he christened 'Little Miss Splendid' and the two rubber boats became a familiar sight nuzzling on the beach as their owners enjoyed picnics, games of cricket and swimming in the clear waters. It became clear that Bingley was completely crazy about Jane. He was attentive and kind, always having a towel ready for her when she emerged shivering from the sea, offering a hand to help her to her feet after sunbathing may have made her dizzy and in a daring moment applying Factor 50 suncream to protect her snowy white back. Jane was cheerful and composed in response, so no-one could guess which way her affections lay.

Lizzy remarked on Jane's strength of character to Lottie one day as they wondered down the beach towards the Venus café for a quiet Magnum and was surprised by her friend's response.

'Jane's behaviour might be admirable in your eyes but she is playing a dangerous game.'

'What do you mean?' asked Lizzy astonished. 'A dangerous game? Are you suggesting Bingley is not what he seems? Is he some sort of criminal or undercover agent who means to trick dear Jane into a sub-culture of espionage or…'

'Lizzy! Be serious. I simply mean that if Jane is so guarded in her behaviour she may lose that which she most desires! Bingley is clearly head over heels in love with Jane but if she shows him no encouragement it may go no further. She must help him on.'

'But if I can tell she has a high regard for him, he must be a simpleton indeed not to discover it too.'

'Lizzy you have known Jane since the cradle. Bingley has only just become aware of her charms.'

'And it is up to him to discover her feelings'

'Perhaps if he sees enough of her. But remember there are always crowds of sisters around. Jane should ensure that she contrives at least some time in his company alone. When she is secure of him, there will be leisure for falling in love as much as she chooses.'

'Fine if her only desire is to be well married. But she has known him barely a fortnight and may not be sure yet of her own feelings. She has swum with him several times a Mill Bay and has visited Captain Morgan's twice with him for a slap up breakfast, The Winking Prawn three times to enjoy a dozen king prawns for lunch and snuggled up in the oak beamed Victoria Inn four times for a fireside supper - but all in company. This is not quite enough to make her understand his character.'

'Not as you represent it. Had she merely visited a public house with him it would be enough to ascertain whether he preferred Becks or Stella Artois; but you must remember that four evenings have also been spent in an intimate atmosphere together – and four evenings may do a great deal.'

'Yes; those four evenings have enabled them to ascertain that they both like Vampire Weekend better than Glasvegas; but with respect to any other leading characteristic, I do not imagine that much has been unfolded.'

'Well,' said Lottie ' I wish Jane success with all my heart and if she were married to him tomorrow, I should think she had as good a chance of happiness, as if she were to be studying his character for a twelve-month.'

So occupied was Lizzy in observing Mr Bingley's attentions to her sister that she failed to notice that she was becoming the object of some interest in the eyes of his friend Mr Darcy. Darcy who had initially dismissed Lizzy had become alarmed that with further observation where he had at first seen fault he now saw strengths. Her face, that he had so criticised, he now saw was rendered uncommonly intelligent by the beautiful expression of her dark eyes. Her manners, though not fashionable by Bingley's sisters standards, were of a light and playful manner that could not fail to attract. In short Darcy, despite himself, was falling in love.

It was at Sir William Lucas's barbeque bash that very evening that Darcy found himself wishing to become better acquainted with Elizabeth. It was a warm and balmy evening. Sir William, had assiduously completed his health and safety check before guests arrived and had placed the barbeque on an upper level of terrace and carefully put red and white tape around the steps leading to it to ensure no-one should venture into such dangerous territory without his permission.

Signs alerted guests to the uneven nature of the pavings, the drop to the side into the estuary, the fact that the sausages might be hot so to wait at least three minutes before biting, and that drinks were limited to two each to avoid unpleasant side effects. With great pleasure and professionalism, Sir William generously gave a little health and safety speech once all the guests were gathered to advise them on dangers and precautions necessary and then bade them to enjoy themselves, but not excessively.

Lydia and Kitty failed to head the final warning of 'not excessively' and were on a mission to enjoy themselves a great deal. Barbeque parties in Salcombe were a thing to be treasured, grasped and revelled in. Some of the more chavvy young guests, who had joined the party only by slipping through a hole in the social net of the Lucas invitation list, feared possible limitations on alcohol from Sir William, so prepared themselves by frontloading before arrival. Fortunately the facility to vom over the sea wall meant the indiscretions of this minority passed largely unnoticed by the majority.

Lydia and Kitty were by no means of this category but once at the party gaily ignored the limit on two drinks and were soon singing, dancing and laughing outrageously loudly with the clutch of handsome young men who had excessive thatches of blond hair or spiky black hair, wore pink shirts with the collars turned up and tails out, long shorts that fell off their waists and balanced dangerously on skinny hips looking as if they might slip further with the slightest provocation and to Sir William's disgust soft shoes with no socks – a smelly result at best, a health hazard at worst But still; he was in no mood to complain. He was the host after all and was all smiles as the young people partied hard around him. He was surprised but delighted that Mr Darcy had deigned to come along.

'Is this not a pleasant evening?' Sir William ventured 'It is always such a joy to see young people enjoying themselves – and…,' he continued observing a young man breakdancing '… how well they dance.'

'Any savage can dance,' retorted Darcy.

At that moment Lizzy happened to step to one side to avoid being kicked in the teeth by the breakdancer and found herself directly before Sir William and Darcy.

'Ah Elizabeth!' said Sir William. 'Mr Darcy and I were just discussing the pleasures of dancing. What a perfect opportunity for you too to show your prowess on the dance floor.'

Mr Darcy though surprised was not adverse to taking Elizabeth as a partner, although breakdancing was not his forte.

'Do not suppose I stepped this way hoping for a partner,' said Elizabeth quickly.

Mr Darcy acknowledged this but reiterated Sir Williams suggestion that they might dance. Lizzy was determined in her refusal and moved away. Darcy's eyes followed her lithe figure as she threaded her way through the gyrating bodies.

'Hmmm' a voice at his shoulder failed to avert his gaze.

'I can guess the subject of your reverie.'

It was Cazza Bingley.

'I should imagine not.'

'I think you are wishing to escape such a grotesque party?'

'You are quite wrong. I was meditating on the very great pleasure which a pair of fine eyes in the face of a pretty woman can bestow.'

'And who is the owner of these 'fine eyes'?'

'Miss Elizabeth Bennet.'

'Miss Elizabeth Bennet! Why I am all astonishment. When are we to wish you joy?'

Mr Darcy allowed Cazza to continue in such a vein. He meanwhile spent the rest of the evening in pleasant observation.

Chapter Seven

THE following day great excitement was felt as it was rumoured a pack of lifeguards were descending on the seaside town where they would be staying to attend training exercises. The girls – and especially Kitty and Lydia - could think of nothing but rippling torsos encased in yellow T-shirts and muscular thighs locked in red shorts. Tales of bravery and rescue were the most enchanting of conversations. After listening to their prattling on this subject Mr Bennet put down the Daily Telegraph and coolly observed.

'From your conversation, you must be the silliest girls in the country. I have suspected it for some time, but I am now convinced.'

'How could you say such a thing about your own daughters?' retorted Mrs Bennet. 'They are not foolish! Indeed they are clever. Why they are all 'A' class students and will all go to excellent universities I'll be bound.'

'Universities? My dear I thought you were only concerned with husbands,' said Mr Bennet, feigning surprise. 'But now you mention it,' he continued turning his attention to Lizzy 'with Jane considering History of Art as a suitable course for a young lady, have you made your decision yet? Do you have a subject? A place of learning? Your room seems piled high in prospectus ... or should that be prospectii?'

'Durham is a possibility, father,' replied Lizzy.

'Durham! Why Durham? It is a cold far flung place that will enable you to escape your sisters but is that a good enough reason?'

'That is not my reason father. It is one of the best universities, with a fine department and to top it all, with it' medieval castle and cathedral, they say it is very pretty.'

'Hmmm. Well visit it first my dear. You don't want to be disappointed.'

'Oh!' A screech from Jane who was sitting before her

Apple laptop made all heads turn.

'What is it my dear?' asked Mrs Bennet.

'An email, mother. From Cazza Bingley.'

'What does it say? Read it out!'

'Hey Jane. Lulu, Hattie and I are so bored right now. Chas has gone off surfboarding. We are marooned here in Netherpollock. Come to munch at lunch with us b4 we go bonkers! Muchos love Cazza :) '

'You must go directly,' said Mrs Bennet excited.

'Shall I take Angelica?'

'No,' retorted her mother. 'It looks like a storm might be brewing. Sail across in the topper and then you will get marooned at East Portlemouth and will have to stay the night.'

Within half an hour Jane was ready to go. She had on a flimsy dress on top of which she wore a bright orange bulky life-jacket which slightly spoilt the delicate effect of the dress but even Mrs Bennet did not want her daughter to actually drown. As she was pushed off from Yeoward and Dowey's jetty the sun was still ominously shining but Mrs Bennet was reassured to see thunderous black clouds thickening on the horizon. By the time Jane was in the centre of the estuary a massive storm had blown up. Later Lizzy was not surprised to receive a message on her phone.

'Lizzie. Got soaked. Whacked on head by boom. Knocked unconscious but picked up by passing fisherman while floating face down in sea. Been to Plymouth hospital. Twenty head stitches for large gash, broken jaw and arm in plaster. Back at Bingley's. Staying night. nbd. Hugs. Jane xx'

On relating this news to the rest of the family Mr Bennet was able to comfort his wife.

'At least if Jane were to die you could feel it was all in pursuit of Mr Bingley.'

'Jane will not die!' said Mrs Bennet indignantly. 'She just has a little scratch. Lizzy, what are you doing?'

'I am going to visit Jane.'

'But why are you putting on your wetsuit?'

'I am going to swim across. The freezing water will do me good.'

'Swim! You will not be fit to be seen.'

'I will be fit to be seen by Jane and that is all that matters.'

'I admire the active form of your benevolence,' observed Mary looking up from Advanced Physics III, 'but every impulse of feeling should be guided by reason; and in my opinion, exertion should always be in proportion to what is required.'

Lizzy could hear nothing as she had now added a rubber head protector and along with flippers, mask and snorkel was making her way out of the front door, down Island Street and descending into the water. It was icy in the sea but Lizzy relished the challenge striking out and cutting her way through waves with impatient activity, and finding herself at last within view of the shore, with weary limbs she crawled up Small's Cove. She was pleased to see all the Bingley party, apart from Jane, assembled before a windshield. Her appearance as an unidentified swimmer emerging from the water caused great surprise and confusion as she tried, possibly in error, to explain her errand before removing her mask and snorkel and making her identity clear. That she should have swum alone across such waters seemed incredible to Cazza, Lulu and Hattie and Lizzy was convinced that they held her in contempt for it. But she was greeted with politeness by them all and by more than politeness by Bingley who went into spasms of 'Splendid! Delightful! Splendid!' to her every remark. Mr Darcy said very little and Mr Hurst, Hattie's overweight boyfriend, said nothing at all. The former was full of admiration for the dripping wet form before him, watching the rivulets of water stream from her hair and down the rubber clad body. The latter was thinking only of his pre-lunch snifter.

Cazza with all generosity took Lizzy up to the house to where Jane was lying in the guest room.

'She has not slept well I am afraid. She is still feverish and has not left her room.'

Upon entering Lizzy could entirely comprehend her sister's inability for exertion. Her beautiful face was barely visible wrapped in a swathe of bandages that covered her from head to toe, her right arm was held aloft in plaster and what Jane had not alerted Lizzy to in her text, not wanting to alarm her, was the broken leg that now pointed to the heavens, held up in traction.

'Oh my dear Jane!' exclaimed Lizzy. 'You are not well.'

Jane's one visible eye spoke volumes so the two sisters sat in silence for some time until Jane dropped into a merciful sleep.

Lizzy returned downstairs where the rest of the party had now gathered for afternoon tea. It was quickly ascertained that Jane was not yet well enough to leave and the suggestion was made that Lizzy should stay at Netherpollock to help speed her sister's recovery. Lizzy accepted with alacrity, and Bingley was dispatched in Little Miss Splendid to collect some attire from 3 Island Street for Lizzy, so she could change out of her wetsuit.

Chapter Eight

AT dinner Lizzy looked radiant in cropped jeans and a smart pale blue and white Crew shirt. Civil enquiries poured in with regards to the patient who, by the ladies, was then soon forgotten restoring Lizzy to her original dislike of them.

Bingley's contrasting constant thoughts for Jane however, endeared her still more to him although even in her own mind his attentions were verging on the excessive. 'Do you think her right eye will recover to its former glory? Of course, *I* don't mind for her left eye is more than beautiful enough for one person but I would not like *her* to be upset.' And 'Oh how gracefully she walked previously – I do pray for *her* sake she will not develop a limp – although of course *I* should not mind, only mind for her sake.' And 'Oh how she had the voice of an angel. Do you think she will be able to speak as sweetly as before? Of course *I* would not mind if she had no voice at all as her angelic looks are enough for me but it might inconvenience *her*.' And 'What if her right arm should not mend? Would she be able to paint and draw and do embroidery as well as previously? Of course, *I* would not mind, her left arm is quite delightful enough for me, but it might upset *her* to be so encumbered.' And so on and so forth until Lizzy barely knew which part of Jane's body had not been discussed and wished for total recovery.

Mr Darcy said little but continued to observe and Mr Hurst simply ate.

After dinner Lizzy returned to Jane who, by blinking with her one visible eye, managed to indicate she was feeling a little better.

Downstairs Cazza, Lulu and Hattie amused themselves by discussing their horror at Lizzy's cross estuary swim.

'Why must she be frolicking about in the waves like that just because her sister had met with a slight misfortune? Her hair so untidy, so blowsy!'

'And her fingers and toes blue with cold. Quite blue!'

'All lost on me,' said Bingley. 'I thought Lizzy looked remarkably well when she emerged from the sea this morning. Her blue extremities quite escaped my notice.'

'You observed it, Mr Darcy, I am sure and I am afraid that this this adventure has rather affected your admiration of her fine eyes.'

'Not at all,' he replied, 'even through her mask I could see that they were brightened by the exercise.'

Cazza was brought to a momentary silence by this remark but then continued, 'Jane is a sweet girl and I hope she will be married well. But with such parentals and such low connections, I am afraid there is no chance of it.'

'No. And what is more they are state educated. They have little hope.'

'State educated they may be but grammar girls,' cried Bingley. 'By my understanding they are as bright as buttons!'

'That, dear brother, is *your* understanding.'

At that moment Lizzy re-entered the room.

'Ah Lizzy! Do come and join us on our Wii,' said Cazza leaping up. 'We thought we would play polo. You are familiar with polo I presume?'

'Sadly not. At our school netball was the main sport. I was wing defence. No I shall decline polo and would rather read.'

'Read!' cried Mr Hurst astonished. 'How could you prefer to read than play polo?'

'Lizzy is a great reader,' said Cazza. 'She is insanely keen on reading, reading, reading, page after page after page, book after book after book and has no pleasure in anything else.'

'That is not true! I …'

'I am sorry I have so pifflingly small a library,' interjected Bingley. 'I am afraid I am not a great reader myself so have only a few classics for you to peruse – Grisham, Fleming, Blyton the usual stuff.'

'I am sure you have a fine library aboard Pemberley Darcy,' said Cazza. 'Your father was a beast of a reader.'

'I do'

'And tell me, will your sweet sister Georgiana be joining us soon? She must be much grown. GCSE's I do believe. And such a bright girl – top of her class at a top *public* school. And what accomplishments – polo of course, and she plays the keyboard like a trooper.'

Chapter Nine

THE following day Lizzy was horrified to see Mrs Bennet, Lydia and Kitty landing at Small's Cove and making their way up the cliff path to Netherpollock. Mrs Bennet was pleased to discover that Jane was not in any danger and so had no wish for her to recover more quickly than necessary and wished instead to prolong her daughter's stay.

Bingley invited them to join them for morning coffee, an invitation Mrs Bennet accepted with alacrity.

'Do you have hot chocolate?' enquired Lydia. 'I was freezing to death on the boat. My fingers are like icebergs.'

'Of course! Hot chocolate it is,' smiled Bingley.

'And how do you like Salcombe Mr Bingley?' enquired Mrs Bennet. 'I do hope we will have the pleasure of your company down here for many a summer to come.'

'Oh it is the most splendid, delightful, splendid location!' enthused Bingley. 'Why I could spend the rest of my days here!'

'And how about you Mr Darcy?'

'I prefer my boat which gives me the opportunity to move on.'

'Is the company not good enough for you here?'

'In a small town the company is naturally less varied than in a larger.'

'I'll have you know Mr Darcy that we keep a good range of company here; most varied and all with manners! We picnic often, for instance with Sir William Lucas – such a man of fashion! so genteel and so easy! He has always something to say to everybody – That is my idea of good breeding; and those persons who fancy themselves very important and never open their mouths, quite mistake the matter.'

An embarrassed silence ensued until Lydia remembering reminded Mr Bingley of his promise to give a beach party.

'I am perfectly ready to keep my promise and as soon a your dear sister has recovered you may name the date and the party will be set.'

Lydia and Kitty squeaked in delight and to Lizzy's relie left with their mother before any more damage could be done

Chapter Ten

THE Bingley party had became particularly fond of The Ferry Inn, which lay on the waterside directly across the estuary from Netherpollock. Evening entertainment saw them take to the seas in Little Miss Splendid to cross the harbour and enjoy the real ale and other liquid refreshments available at this lively inn.

It meant leaving the invalid, Jane, still in traction on the other side of the waters, but they supplied her with a torch and it was felt that if the pain worsened and that she was in mortal danger or in need of extra morphine she could always signal across by flashing in morse code.

Lizzy was amused to note on these occasions how outrageously Cazza would flirt with Darcy, complimenting him on his speed of texting ('I text rather slowly' came the reply), how masterfully he managed Little Miss Splendid's tiller, ('No better than any other man before me.') and what fine taste he had in beers ('I assure you, selecting a pint of Marston's Pedigree does not make me a connoisseur').

Karaoke was always leapt upon as a great diversion and Cazza, Lulu and Hattie delighted the locals in a bawdy rendition of 'Je t'aime' but Lizzy could not be prevailed upon. Darcy tried to encourage her to join in some arm wrestling but she was not to be drawn. However, her sweet and fun loving nature was having an effect. Darcy was bewitched.

Chapter Eleven

FRANTIC morse coding from across the bay went unnoticed at The Ferry Inn until the group were departing and became aware of a flashing light. On landing on Small's Cove, Lizzy leapt out of Little Miss Splendid and hurried up the cliff path to Jane's room whereupon she found her sister had fallen out of bed and had become entangled in the traction equipment.

'I am sorry,' said Jane gasping through a web of bandages that had come loose. 'I was merely trying to get to the window to send a morse code message as I was ravaged with pain. Oh!'

It was only now that Lizzy realised the folly of their plan: Jane's torch could not be shone through the window at the correct angle to be seen at The Ferry Inn if she was lying in her bed. It was an unfortunate mistake. As Lizzy was pondering the error Cazza, Lulu and Hattie popped their heads round the door and claimed delight that Jane seemed to be recovering so speedily then dashed downstairs to watch reality TV. Lizzy remained to heave Jane back into bed, re-tie her bandages, including strapping up the broken jaw which as a consequence left her dear sister unable to speak again and re-setting the traction, before descending to the drawing room, by which time the news had come on and Cazza, yawning, suggested she and Lizzy took a turn on the treadmills.

'I assure you it is very refreshing after sitting so long in one attitude.'

Lizzy accepted happily and the young ladies started jogging 2km at a speed of 11.5. Darcy looked up at the spectacle and Cazza immediately asked him to join them.

'Try the rowing machine Darcy. You have the perfect physic for rowing.'

Darcy declined and spent the rest of the evening exercising his vision in a most pleasing fashion.

Chapter Twelve

THE next day, despite Mrs Bennet's protestations the elder Bennet girls decided the time had come to return to 3 Island Street and Angelica was sent for. Jane was stretchered down the step cliff path swaddled in bandages and deposited in the loyal inflatable. Lizzy waved goodbye to the Netherpollock party with relief and Jane blinked repeatedly in gratitude, leaving the two young men, Bingley and Darcy, on the beach, feeling deflated by the departure of their recent acquaintances. Bingley remained on the sands waving until Angelica and its precious cargo was out of sight; Darcy muttered an expletive and turned to walk at a fearsome pace across rugged cliff paths determined to beat out unwelcome passions.

Chapter Thirteen

THE following week saw the Town Regatta commence in Salcombe. This was a week of uncommon excitement and challenging events. Running races, street art, fancy dress were all on offer but for the Bennet girls the highlights had to be the Estuary Swim and the Greasy Pole competition.

Jane was recovering well though Mary insisted she still bore a convincing resemblance to the Egyptian mummy, Queen Hatshepsut. Mummy or not, Mr Bennet was relieved to have his two elder girls home. The remainder of his family had done their very best to drive him insane with their constant chitter-chatter about hunky lifeguards, rugged fishermen and brave and bold lifeboatmen. He had one further reason to be glad of their return of which we will now hear.

'Mrs Bennet,' he said, 'I hope you will make a special visit to obtain fresh lobster today from a local pot as we have a visitor for dinner tonight.'

'But we are partying father!' interrupted Lydia in dismay. It's Honky's birthday and he has invited all the beautiful young people to meet at Whitestrand at six and then we're walking over to North Sands to chill out on the beach for a bit before having cracked crab in The Winking Prawn. How awesome is that?'

'Tonight, Lydia, you will dine with us,' interjected Mr Bennet with unusual firmness. 'I have received a letter from a gentleman and a stranger.'

The pairing of the words held the young lady's attention momentarily.

'It's Mr Bingley!' cried Mrs Bennet. 'Why Jane did you say nothing of it?'

'It is not Mr Bingley,' said Mr Bennet with patience. 'It is from my cousin, Mr Collins, who, when I am dead may turn you all out of Longbourn and 3 Island Street as soon as he pleases!'

'Oh that odious man!' exclaimed Mrs Bennet. 'I cannot bear to hear his name! How unfair it is that he should inherit our family's wealth and leave our girls penniless!'

'We will not be penniless mother for we are educated and are going to university and will, God willing, have a career.'

'A career! A career! What do I care for a career?' wailed Mrs Bennet. 'All I care for is to see my five daughters well married for they will inherit nothing. Nothing!'

'Calm yourself, my dear,' commanded Mr Bennet 'Let me read you an extract from his letter which may perhaps soften you towards him.'

'Dear Sir, sorry about the mix-up between our papas Mine has now gone to a better place and I, having recently been ordained, find myself quite dashing in a dog collar and in a good spot, fiscally speaking and thinking outside the box (or kennel!) would be more than happy to touch base with you and your daughters to heal the chasm and since my boss Lady Catherine de Brrr has condescended to see me married off I will hasten to you and arrive at six.

Yours William C'

At six o'clock Mr Collins did indeed arrive. He had an excessive number of bags and was unable to find a space for his car. This caused him great anxiety as he did not want to b issued with a parking ticket as firstly, it was not seemly for a vicar to be reprimanded in such a manner and secondly Lady Catherine de Brrr would be seriously displeased. Mary stepped forward to offer her services and guided the distressed guest to the Batson Creek car park where he failed to have the right amount of change but Mary again was happy to help and demonstrated the method of being able to easily dispose of a large number of coins into the machine.

Once Mr Collins was successfully located in his room on the second floor of the little terraced house, Lydia made a general announcement at the top of her voice that they should hurry, for the Greasy Pole competition was about to take place.

Mr Collins was anxious to accompany the girls and had already spied that Jane seemed exceedingly pretty and commented to Mrs Bennet as he passed her in the hall that he thought her eldest daughter would make an excellent Mrs Collins.

'You flatter us Mr Collins with your kind attentions,' replied Mrs Bennet in a whisper, 'but I should tell you that Jane is practically engaged.'

'Oh!' Mr Collins looked crestfallen but then, after a moments thought, transferred his affections to Elizabeth and - as far as he was concerned - all was well.

'Come *on!*' urged Lydia.

Mary attempted to walk with Mr Collins along the small path that took them round to the quayside where a large crowd was gathering but Mr Collins seemed anxious to sidle up to Lizzy. He eventually found himself in what seemed to be a queue and although he devoted himself to interesting conversation felt the attentions of the young ladies were not with him and something was going on which he was not really party to.

Ahead there was a great deal of noise, shouting, laughing and rather unnervingly for Mr Collins, splashing. He soon became aware that the queue was moving slowly but undeniably towards the edge of the water but he still could not quite make out what was going on.

Suddenly and to his horror he saw that Lydia was pulling off her strappy top, which he had already considered immodest, and then worse, peeling off her excessively short skirt and the rest of her sisters were following suit, even Lizzy, the object of his affections. The five girls now stood before him, all in the skimpiest of bikinis, apart from Jane who still had plaster on arms and legs and Mary who wore a more modest all in one swimsuit and was now tucking her short hair into an unbearably tight fitting bathing cap.

'Come along Mr Collins,' cried Kitty laughing. 'Get your kit off!'

'I will most certainly not! What would Lady Catherine think?'

'Oh hurry up!' said Lydia impatiently and she grabbed at Mr Collins' shorts. Before he knew it he was standing in his Y-fronts shivering on the quayside.

'I say! This is outrageous! Give me back my clothes!'

'Too late. It's your go!' cried Kitty in delight.

Mr Collins found himself now at the front of the queue and before him a long pole, about the width of a telegraph pole was extended, horizontally, out over the water. At the end of the extrusion, which was greased for extra slipperiness, to his amazement sat Lydia, practically naked, laughing and shrieking.

On the safe land side a jolly middle-aged woman, fully dressed, ushered Mr Collins onto the pole.

'Off you go. See if you can knock the young lady off!'

The true horror of the situation now unfolded to the unhappy clergyman. About one hundred people stood lining the quayside. About fifty more were bobbing around in the water. With great caution Mr Collins sat down on the pole legs dangling each side and edged his flabby, white body along and out over the sea.

'Oh my! Oh my!' he muttered involuntarily, finding the constant lurching forward exceedingly uncomfortable an more than a little painful.

'Come on!' shrieked Lydia.

After several agonising minutes during which he nearly lost his balance several times Mr Collins found himself face to face with Lydia.

'On your marks, get set, go!' commanded the woman from the safety of the bank.

Lydia swung her right arm at Mr Collins who by chance sneezed and in doing so ducked. Lydia was caught off balance and with a shriek fell into the sea. Mr Collins was the victor! A cheer went up from the spectators. It was all over so quickly.

'Turn around!' came the command from the shore.

With colossal difficulty Mr Collins heaved his ungainly body around to face back to shore. Once round he looked up and saw Lizzy herself, the object of his affections, edging towards him along the pole, delightful in her blue, polka dot bikini.

'Oh my Lord' breathed Collins. 'Oh my! Oh my!'

Lizzy got closer and closer.

'On your marks, get set, go!' commanded the woman from the side once more.

With pudgy fingers Mr Collins grabbed hold of Lizzy's arms and she his, trying to push him into the sea, so for a moment or two they rocked from side to side until suddenly all balance was lost and they fell, still locked in each other's arms into the salty waters.

They rose spluttering, Mr Collins gasping for breath, Lizzy almost drowning in her hilarity. Along the bank a cheer and roar of laughter went up from the spectators, only superseded by an even greater cheer and roar of laughter as a pair of Y-fronts was, a few moments later, seen floating on the surface.

Chapter Fourteen

LATER that evening, during dinner with the family Mr Collins attempted to re-gain his dignity and personal sense of importance. He began by directing his first remarks in a suitably formal manner to Mr Bennet.

'Mr Bennet, I do not presume to come to this thy table trusting in my own righteousness but in thy manifold ...'

'Oh there is no need for that!' interjected Mrs Bennet not quite following Mr Collins's train of thought but feeling he was unnecessarily apologising for something.

'My dear, you have interrupted an important speech!' chided Mr Bennet, much amused. 'Mr Collins, pray do go on.'

'Thy manifold ... er ... great and many, many manifolds ... and ... oh mercy!'

Mr Collins had little idea of what he was going to say in the first place and had launched out by using familiar words which now he started to feel were out of context. He was sure he had heard them *somewhere* before. Whilst he was pondering this a silence fell over the table only broken by a sudden exclamation from Lydia.

'Oh Lor! There seem to be some crumbs under the table. Gather them up Kitty!'

Girlish laughter spilled over and Mr Collins confused and perplexed, felt the moment had come to redirect the conversation to a subject of which he was certain of his expertise. With this mind and to the delight of Mr Bennet, Mr Collins talked with great eloquence, longevity and deference about his patron Lady Catherine de Brrr, her admirable condescension and her daughter who by not being presented at Court had deprived Britain of its brightest ornament.

Chapter Fifteen

THE following day the girls set off on a mission to North Sands to investigate the lifeguard training rumour. If a pack of lifeguards were in the vicinity the girls were naturally most anxious to make their acquaintance and, having taken care with their appearances, set off in good spirits from 3 Island Street. Their only distress was that Mr Collins had decided to accompany them and had been encouraged by Mr Bennet, who was finding the entertainment value of the foibles of this foolish man wearing thin. And so the party set off through town, past the children crabbing on Victoria Quay, up Fore Street, where they stopped every minute or so to dive into Cranch's for gobstoppers, or the Salcombe Dairy for a tutti-frutti ice-cream, or Joules, or Crew, or Musto, or Jack Wills or White Stuff or Fat Face to check on the latest hoodies or to enjoy a few girly moments in Amelia's Attic heaven, tempted by beautiful strings of freshwater pearls and life saving little books on how to look as gorgeous as a goddess, so it took them quite a good half-hour before they had even reached the Yacht Club. Mr Collins begged them to stop for a moment to admire the view and also give himself the opportunity to get his breath back. But the girls were now impatient to get on and so with Mr Collins puffing and panting behind they gambled forth, passed Windcot, a delightful home which often opened it's gardens to the public and where Mr Bennet had in mind a peaceful retirement and then down the hill again to North Sands.

Quite a sight met their eyes. The beach was strewn with young lifeguards, dressed in yellow RNLI Lifeguard T-shirts and red shorts, practising a number of exercises from dragging one another up and down the beach to pumping inert friends on the chest.

'Oh look!' cried Kitty. 'There is Denny! He said he was going on this course after dropping out of uni' … but who is that with him? He's an absolute machine!'

'Denny! Denny!'

Kitty and Lydia rushed down to the beach whereupon they were soon introduced to the handsome stranger.

'This,' said Denny, 'is my good friend Mr Wickham who has recently joined up after having an equally disastrous affair at uni'as – hey Wickham!'

The said Wickham chose to ignore Denny's comments and proved himself to be all wit, charm and quite delightful to the five Bennet girls. He flexed his muscles and gave them such a detailed explanation of mouth to mouth resuscitation that they were left feeling quite breathless. Just as he had put them in recovery position on the sparkling sand who should chance upon the beach but Mr Bingley and Mr Darcy. Bingley looked quite the holiday maker in his stripped Bermuda shorts, Ray-Ban sunglasses and brightly coloured towel gaily slung over his smooth white shoulder. Darcy had on a similar outfit but the colours were more subdued and he retained his blue and white striped cotton shirt, unbuttoned which revealed a thatch of dark, curling hairs.

'Mr Bingley!' shouted Lydia 'Do come and look! We are all in recovery.'

Bingley, delighted at chancing upon the girls, strode across with Darcy in tow. Despite the protection of wearing Tom Ford sunglasses with smoke blue lenses, Darcy had to control himself from staring at Lizzy who was lying between Jane and Mary. His affection for her was becoming uncomfortably strong. Her bikini clad body was almost too much and he fought hard not to give anything of his feelings away. Bingley he considered was making a regular fool of himself by conversing with Jane at ground level, for her convenience, his hair flopping onto the sand. So Darcy stared steadfastly out to sea and tried to think of anything but the female form. One moment of weakness however allowed his gaze to fall again upon the enticing Lizzy and in doing so he spotted Wickham. Wickham at the same moment caught sight of Darcy and Lizzy observing both, could not help notice that one turned red and the other white and were barely able to acknowledge one another. Bingley meanwhile was regretfully bidding his farewells to Jane as he had boat business to attend to and called to Darcy to come along.

Lizzy was meanwhile left mystified. Wickham and Darcy had definitely recognised each other but it was not a happy meeting. What could be the meaning of their exchange?

Chapter Sixteen

LIZZY'S curiosity was soon to be satisfied. Once the official training session was complete, the lifeguards took it upon themselves to organise a riotous game of volleyball, which her younger sisters joined in with gusto. The lifeguards, now off duty, stripped off their yellow shirts to reveal a range of fine torsos. The girls, most already in bikinis had no further garments to strip off and the game started immediately. The lifeguards, though clearly the better players were gentlemen at heart and encouraged the girls to leap and run for the ball, snatching it from them at the last moment causing many a shriek and a tumble and a fumble in the sands. Meanwhile Mary was complaining the sun was too hot, despite wearing a bonnet, and so Jane, kindness as always, offered to accompany her to The Winking Prawn where they could enjoy a cool lemonade and recover in the shade.

Lizzy, in thoughtful mood, wondered over to the rocks to explore a little, hoping to catch a common limpet off guard and prize it momentarily off it's foundations or to enjoy watching the sea anemones waving in the shallow waters.

'Is that a beadlet?'

An amiable, pleasant-sounding voice made her jump and almost lose her footing. A firm hand grabbed her arm to steady her and she looked up to find herself staring into the merry eyes of Mr Wickham.

'Oh Mr Wickham! You made me start! Are you not playing volleyball?'

'No. I would much prefer to seek out treasures over here. I have always loved rock pools since I was a small boy and take every opportunity I can to come to tease out lovely limpets and pretty periwinkles.'

To Lizzy's surprise she acknowledged he must be telling the truth for, in his other hand, not the one that still held her arm so charmingly, he held a fishing net and bucket.

The two were soon crouched down over pools, delighting in their finds when the conversation turned, by Wickham's initiation, to Darcy. He inquired how long Mr Darcy had been in Salcombe.

'About a week or so. He has a beast of a yacht here – the Pemberley.'

'Yes. He has a fat wallet indeed. In fact, you could not have met with a person more capable of giving you such information – for I have been connected with his family from my Pampers' days.'

Lizzy was all astonishment.

'Yes, you may look surprised. It is a sorry tale of events which I will not tire you with. Mr Darcy's father was the most amiable of men, who, when my fortunes suffered a blow as a child, took me in and brought me up as his own. Darcy I'm afraid was horribly jealous. His padre had always wished me to follow into the family business but when a place became vacant I am afraid old Mr Darcy had already passed away and young Darcy gave the position to another. I was left penniless but I managed to scrimp and save, go to uni' where … well here I am!'

'But that is outrageous! What disgraceful behaviour of Darcy. I thought ill of him before but this is too much!'

Lizzy looked so angry and put out that Wickham felt quite sorry for her.

'Don't be upset on my behalf! A young man these day

44

should have to make his own way. I see it as a great fortune that I have not had too much handed on a plate. Unlike Darcy I am a free man. The world is my oyster!' And with that he held up a periwinkle as if an oyster and, looking directly at Lizzy, added, '… and who knows what pearls I might find.'

Chapter Seventeen

TUESDAY was the long awaited Salcombe Estuary Swim. Bingley who had promised a breakfast party on this day had been forced to change his plans, having been unaware that he would be clashing with such an auspicious local occasion.

The night before, the Bennet girls had met in The King's Arms with a number of their Salcombe friends. Lydia was at full throttle.

'I shall not bother with a wetsuit. It is such a bore trying to pull it on and off all the time and it makes me look like a giant seal. No I shall wear the skimpiest of bikinis so all the lifeguards will make sure of rescuing me should I get into difficulties.'

'I must have goggles though,' interrupted Kitty. 'I can't like see a thing without goggles.'

'Although I have great demands on my intellect to continue my studies I feel an early morning swim can but only help. I will be coming but I feel a wise approach is necessary for a successful outcome. I shall wear goggles and my all-in-one Billabong wetsuit,' announced Mary.

'Will you be taking to the waters, Mr Collins?' asked Lizzy teasingly. 'Or would it be considered too unseemly for a man of your position? I am sure you would not want word to get back to Lady Catherine de Brrr of any outrageous behaviour!'

Mr Collins was appalled by the idea of having to swim across the estuary at seven o'clock in the morning. He had, however, enjoyed a glass of wine or two and also being in courting mode felt an unaccustomed bravado come over him.

'Lady Catherine would want her vicar to lead by example. I will certainly be there and if I may take the opportunity to ask if *you*, Lizzy, would care to sit next to me on the boat going over so that I may protect you from any undesirable spray, and that I might then have the pleasure of guiding you through any hazardous waters that might come in our way on the swim back.'

Lizzy's heart sank. She had very much hoped to have the pleasure of swimming alongside Mr Wickham. A slow suspicion had been creeping over her that Mr Collins, from amongst her sisters, had shown a preference for her and this latest remark only confirmed her worst fears.

Chapter Eighteen

FISHERMEN, tradesman and early walkers – usually elderly – are generally the only characters to be seen in the very early hours of the morning in Salcombe during the summer months. The holiday-makers take a slow start to the day, luxuriating in the opportunity to stay in bed just that little bit longer unless excited toddlers persuade them to get up early and out on the sands. The latest risers are teenagers and young adults wasted from the previous night's partying or from late night escapades on the beach which have left them in need of extra sleep.

Not so on the morning of the Estuary Swim. By 6.30am black rubber clad figures are creeping out of front doors closing them softly behind. From Devon Road, Shadycombe Road, Church Street, Buckley Street they come – the teenagers joined by the elderly and youngsters – streaming up Fore Street, past Whitestrand, past The Ferry Inn, past the War Memorial and down onto Cliff House Gardens where they gather – not in the twos or threes, not in their tens or twenties but in their hundreds.

The atmosphere intensifies, the Harbour Master and his team are at the ready and the first boat loads of swimmers are taken across the sparkling waters to Small's Cove where they assemble for the big swim back.

All was commotion down in 3 Island Street. Lizzy and Jane were ready wearing cosy hoodies over their swimwear and carrying beach towels. Lydia was hunting for her bikini top and suddenly confessed that she might have left it on North Sands the day before - how it could have come detached she did not know - so wanted to borrow the bikini that Kitty was wearing who said she could not because she already had it on so in the end Lydia had to wear an unmatching top and bottom. Mary was taking an interminable time getting into her Billabong and they were in danger of running late when they all at last were gathered in the tiny hall.

'Ready at last!' said Lydia, her eyes gleaming in excitement.

Lizzy was just about to step onto the street when her heart stopped.

'Mr Collins! Where is Mr Collins? Mary did you wake him? You promised you would.'

Mary already boiling in her wetsuit would have gone redder if she wasn't already bright beetroot.

'I forgot,' she mumbled.

The last thing poor Lizzy wished to happen was for Mr Collins to accompany them on the swim but she felt it would be too unkind to give him the slip so she raced upstairs and knocked on his door. There was no answer. She knocked again. Still no answer. With caution she opened the door and called his name softly and then a little louder. With still no response she started to close the door when suddenly from the bedclothes came a snort, a sniffle and then Mr Collins face turned towards her, his eyes opened and then opened wide.

'Elizabeth! My own Elizabeth! Oh my Lord! You have come! I do doubt the wisdom of your forwardness but I am prepared to forgive you such is my passion for you!'

He threw back the duvet inviting her into his hot and enseamed bed.

'Mr Collins! You forget yourself,' cried Lizzy in much alarm. 'And you forget that today is the Estuary Swim. I have merely come to wake you as Mary has quite forgot. We are leaving now so if you wish to join us please make haste!'

And with that Lizzy turned, shut the door and raced downstairs, her heart beating and her whole being a little shaken by the experience.

'Is he like coming?' asked Kitty, hoping he was not.

In answer to her question a banging of a door and footsteps were heard above and Mr Collins appeared, dishevelled, but attired in surprisingly brief swimming trunks and carrying the wetsuit Mr Bennet had so kindly lent him the night before.

'Sorry ladies to have delayed you but let us not dally now! I am ready for whatever delights lie before us!'

And with that the little party hurried to join the throng at Cliff House Gardens.

Once they had paid their entry fee of £1.00, obtained their numbered rubber wrist band and joined the queue for the boats Lizzy looked around for Wickham. She was disappointed not to see him there but consoled herself thinking he may already be on the far side. Certainly Bingley would already be on the beach with his sisters, as Netherpollock lay that side. It then crossed her mind that if Darcy was going to be there Wickham might deliberately avoid the event. Her anger towards Darcy intensified at the thought.

'Do not be alarmed!' consoled Mr Collins seeing her expression and taking her arm. 'The seas might be treacherous but I will be here to guide you and save you from any peril.'

Mr Collins was attentive to Lizzy from then onwards. He helped her down the steps, nearly causing her to trip and fall; he pushed her onto the boat so that she fell headlong onto the wooden planks; he shielded her from the spray as the crossed so she could see nothing but the fleshy white of his chest and he gallantly leapt out of the boat to help her down on arrival – but anticipated the landing early in error, so they both found themselves chest deep in the icy sea. Mr Collins found himself so short of breath by the dramatic change in temperature that he could scarcely breathe and seemed unable to move, until suddenly he ran shrieking out of the water, then remembering Lizzy turned to help her out, pulling her so she fell again into the sea.

At last all were ashore on Small's Cove and were mingling with four hundred or so other early morning swimmers, all in good spirits, all discussing how cold the water would or would not be and whether it would or would not be advisable to wear a wetsuit.

'My wetsuit!' exclaimed Mr Collins. 'I fear I have left it on the launch!'

'I have it,' said Jane kindly. 'When you so gallantly leapt overboard I picked it up thinking it might be forgotten.'

'Thank you! Thank you!' exalted Mr Collins. 'You are kindness indeed. Even Lady Catherine would condescend to agree that you almost have the same excessive kindness for which she is famous! Thank you again.'

'Would you like some help putting it on?' further queried Jane.

'No. It would not be seemly. I can manage myself thank you,' replied Mr Collins who proceeded to attempt to squeeze himself into the rubbery outfit. It was challenging. Mr Collins soon found himself unbalancing on one leg, rolling round on the sand, trying in vain to catch the zip strap on his back and with more help than he would like to admit to, eventually found himself crammed into the all in one suit. It was not a pretty sight.

Lizzy, meanwhile, scanned the beach, which now resembled a seal colony with its vast numbers of barking, black clad figures. Any moment she expected David Attenborough to leap out of the tall pines which surrounded the beach, microphone in hand, and explain the extraordinary annual migration – although, it has to be said, among the black were an equal number of brave souls who wore only swimming costumes and stood shrieking and shivering. Yet there was, indeed, no sign of Wickham. Denny appeared and Lydia was immediately forthright enough to enquire of his handsome friend.

'Wickham has gone for a run over to Bolt Head. This swim would have been a great pleasure to him but I am afraid he wished to avoid a certain gentleman.'

Lizzy felt her heart harden against Darcy, as her dislike of him was sharpened by the immediate disappointment. But she was not one to sulk and seeing her friend, Lottie Lucas, she was able to discuss her griefs, having to drop the subject as Bingley, his sisters and the detestable Darcy himself joined their group.

'Splendid! Delightful. Absolutely splendid!' enthused Bingley. 'I say, what a perfectly splendid event. I can't wait to get in that sea. Are you a strong swimmer Jane?' And on enquiring he angled himself closer to the young lady in question. Mr Darcy, similarly seemed to be approaching Lizzy, who feeling he was the last person in the world she wished to talk to, moved away and unfortunately found herself shoulder to shoulder with Mr Collins. Mr Collins, uncomfortable and sweating profusely in the ill-fitting wetsuit, took this as a compliment and to Lizzy's horror, put out a rubber paw and held her hand. So shocked was she that she gave out a little squeal which he took to be a squeal of delight and held more firmly so despite her discreet wriggling, she was unable to escape.

There was a ripple of excitement across the beach. The Harbour Master had transferred all contenders; from his wooden boat, twenty yards out to sea he was holding an oar aloft; the sea was choppy but not wild; the tide was high; the early morning sun sparkled: the moment had come.

'When I drop my oar it is the signal to start,' he bellowed

Despite the megaphone nobody could hear his words, yet despite not hearing his words everyone got the gist. Almost. The oar had not quite dropped but everyone knew he was on the verge - the sound of his voice had been enough, excitement overspilled and the several hundred people who had waited so patiently and with such good humour on the beach now ran at full speed into the water.

The splashing was unprecedented, the battle roar tremendous as bodies large and small, fat and thin, old and young hurled themselves voluntarily into the waves. Lydia and Kitty found themselves at the forefront with Denny and a group of six fit young men. Mary, not wishing to be last had allowed herself to be swept along with the crowd and was swimming side-stroke in a regular, balanced motion, trying to recite the periodic table to take her mind off the cold. Bingley had made a dash for it with Jane and they were destined to enjoy a most romantic swim across with the young man feeling he had fallen in love with a mermaid, so beautifully – in his eyes – did the eldest Miss Bennet glide through the water. Lizzy meanwhile was right at the back. Mr Collins had not released his grip of her when the rush began. Being right by the shore as everyone charged in the pair found themselves near the front, but they were soon overtaken.

'Oh it's cold!' shrieked Mr Collins, hopping about, barely toe deep. 'Oh my! Oh my!'

'Come on!' insisted Lizzy impatiently.

Mr Collins was forced to let go of Lizzy's hand as he could not swim *and* be noble, being good at neither. Lizzy waded out and struck off, but her kind heart impelled her to turn to see that Mr Collins was now only waist deep, and still not swimming but bobbing around on tip toes trying not to get wet.

'Oh my! Oh my! I can hardly breath! Oh my!'

'You can swim, can't you?' shouted Lizzy.

'Oh my! Of course! Lady Catherine condescended herself to compliment me on hearing that I achieved my

51

Duckling Award at the tender age of six but ...'

He tripped and lunged forward into the water. Lizzy was not able to tell if he was swimming or floundering. The buoyancy of his wetsuit seemed to keep him roughly afloat but they were going at such a slow pace that the other swimmers were moving away.

'Mr Collins, we will never cross the estuary at this rate. Can you not speed up?'

'I ...! Oh! I think I have swallowed a fish! I ...! Oh my!'

Mr Collins, now progressed to deeper water, was coughing and spluttering, and flailing his arms around and indeed looked in danger of drowning. They were out of their depths and Lizzy had serious cause for concern.

'Oh my! Oh ...'

Mr Collins disappeared under the waters.

'Mr Collins! Mr Collins!' She looked around but there was no sign. She dived under. Nothing could be seen! She dived again. Nothing! It seemed Mr Collins had completely disappeared!

'Help! Help! Over here!' Lizzy waved frantically at the lifeguards who were floating around on surfboards for the very purpose of rescuing anyone in difficulties. But as she waved, she felt a tug on her leg and was pulled underwater. Something black enveloped her pushing her down, deeper and deeper. As it pushed her deeper it propelled itself upwards. Lizzy thought her lungs would burst. Almost too late she escaped the great weight and freed, swam desperately to the surface. Only moments from death she managed to gasp in great mouthfuls of air and even in such desperate straits she was conscious of the sight of the great black posterior of Mr Collins being heaved onto a surfboard and his plaintive cry of 'Oh my! Oh my! I nearly drowned! Oh! Oh! Oh!'

Mr Collins safe and thankfully out of the way, Lizzy now filled her lungs with air and struck out with vigour. She was fine swimmer and was determined, despite this initial set back not to finish last. She sped through the water, doing a fas crawl, enjoying the physical challenge and soon catching up with a clutch of swimmers. At the same time she became aware that someone was swimming alongside her. She paused for breath and on looking round to her astonishment saw it was Mr Darcy! He too was a fine swimmer and seemed able to talk and swim at the same time with ease.

'I do hope you do not mind me accompanying you Miss Bennet?'

'You are hardly alone in accompanying me Mr Darcy. There are at least four hundred other swimmers in the vicinity.'

'I mean swim alongside you?'

'If you wish.'

And Lizzy struck out as fast as she could but to her irritation found that Darcy managed to keep up with her with ease.

They found themselves overtaking Sir William Lucas who was swimming at a cautious rate.

'Ah Lizzy! Darcy!' he puffed. 'This sea is full of young people swimming with such style and grace. Allow me to say, Mr Darcy, your young partner does not disgrace you and I am sustained in my efforts by thoughts of a desirable event, my dear Eliza, that may soon take place.' And he glanced across at Jane and Bingley who were swimming, now at a leisurely pace, just to starboard. Darcy was halted in his tracks by this thought which seemed to strike him forcibly. Uncharacteristically he seemed to loose control and swallow an unwise amount of seawater causing a temporary spluttering and coughing. Lizzy wishing to escape took her chance and swam swiftly on. Yet Darcy, recovered, hastened to catch up again, which to Elizabeth's annoyance, he did and proceeded to encourage conversation whilst swimming on his back.

'What think you of books?'

'Books? I feel we will be all at sea in our varying opinions of books, Mr Darcy.'

'Then let us discuss our opinions.'

'Opinions? I remember you once saying that once you have an opinion of someone you will not change. You must be cautious about forming those opinions.'

'Indeed I am.'

'And you are never blinded by prejudice?'

'I hope not.'

'First impressions must be most important to you. Oh sorry!'

Lizzy's apology came from her error in coming into contact with a rather porky man to her port.

'To what are you alluding?'

'Your character Mr Darcy. I have heard so many conflicting opinions that I am having trouble making you out.'

'I would wish Miss Bennet that you would not sketch my character at present as I have reason to fear that some may not wish to give you the best impression. Owch!'

The portly gentleman swerved to avoid Lizzy and in doing so hit Darcy in a most uncomfortable spot. Darcy for the second time found himself spluttering and gasping - this time in agony and Lizzy, for the second time found an opportunity to escape and merged into a group of swimmers just ahead.

'Oh Lizzy!' came the haughty voice of Lulu. 'I must warn you that your beloved Wickham is not all that he seems. Darcy has always been remarkably kind to him - even though he was only a trumped up ...'

'That is enough Louisa!' retorted Lizzy angrily. 'Wickham himself told me of his background, which it seems is his only crime and *I* will not be prejudiced against him for that reason!'

And with that Lizzy swam off with as much energy as she could muster, not waiting to hear Lulu's 'Oh no need to get all moody!' retort.

Swimmers were now starting to reach land on the town side. Faces glowing, hearts pounding, exuberant in their achievement they climbed the steps out of the sea and into the Cliff House Gardens where they were given a hero's welcome by waiting friends, a Mars bar and prized Harbour Swim Certificate by the organisers. There was no more joyous couple than Jane and Bingley who had swum together for the whole distance and were now only separated as Bingley, happy to see Jane warm in her towel, went to find his.

'Oh lor! Oh lor!' Lydia was shrieking. 'That was a beast of a swim! I was freezing all the way. My fingers are blue.'

'Not half as cold as I was,' said Kitty. 'Look my fingers are bluer than yours.'

'It was horrible! Horrible!' sobbed Mary. 'What a foolish, ill advised idea. I will never again take to the seas. I nearly died!'

'You will recover, I am sure,' said Jane kindly, as she and Lizzy joined the group.

'I say girls! Girls!'

'Oh no! Mr Collins! Whatever is the matter with him?'

'He looks as if he is going to explode!'

'How did he get across so quickly?'

Mr Collins had been relieved to have been rescued early on in the swim and so avoid the physical exertion so enjoyed by most of the remaining four hundred swimmers. He had been delivered by surfboard back to the safety of Cliff House Gardens and had been able to watch the event, wrapped warmly in his towel, and by eavesdropping on some fellow spectators had picked up the most extraordinary news which he was now about to relate to the surprised and shivering Bennet girls.

'I say! I say! I say! News of the most exciting nature! By chance I have discovered that the nephew of my patroness, Lady Catherine de Brrr, is here! Here in Salcombe! And there he is! Right now! Coming out of the water! Fitzwilliam Darcy! What a fine figure of a man! I will go and make his acquaintance!' Mr Collins rushed off, pushing his way down the slippery steps as swimmers endeavoured to come up the steps. Darcy, only just recovered from his agony in the water, was unprepared for the onslaught of friendliness from Mr Collins, who grabbed him in a handshake and had only just managed to get out the words:

'Lady Catherine would be ...' before he slipped, fell from the steps into the deep water pulling the astonished Darcy with him.

The waters closed over them. Lizzy whose embarrassment was overtaken by hilarity now felt a stab of fear as no sign of either men could be seen. Suddenly Darcy emerged.

'Where is the fool?' he shouted, gasping for breath and looking wildly around. Then Darcy disappeared yanked from below as if by a deep sea monster and Mr Collins, in turn appeared.

'Oh my! Oh my! Save me! Lady Catherine would ...'

Mr Collins never finished his sentence as Darcy rose to the surface again and despite Mr Collins's efforts to drown *him*, managed to get them both safely to the steps. The ordeal of a near drowning for the second time in one day had so shocked Mr Collins that he was unable to stand so Darcy was forced to carry him, in his arms, up the steps. Physically Mr Collins succumbed like a baby to this mode of transport. Mentally however, he was quite alert and was not one to miss an opportunity. Recovering slightly he could see the closeness of the situation was the perfect moment for a little intimate conversation and proceeded to wrap his arms fondly around Darcy's neck and to introduce himself.

'Mr Darcy what a fortunate meeting this is. I have reason to believe you are the nephew of my patroness Lady Catherine de Brrr, who ... oh! Oh my! Oh! ...'

Darcy on the verge of exploding, had had enough. He deposited Mr Collins in a blob at the feet of the vicar' cousins and strode off - not before he had unwillingly overheard Mrs Bennet, who had just arrived on the scene expressing in the loudest of voices to Mrs Lucas how she was looking forward to a happy event between her eldest daughter and the charming Mr Bingley. The past few moments had been mortifying for Lizzy but worse was to come. Mary had managed to inveigle herself with the organisers and to Lizzy's horror had volunteered to give a vote of thanks on behalf of the swimmers. Mary had climbed onto a table and was trying to master the megaphone with little success.

'Oh behalf of the ...' beep ' I would like to ...' screech. All the swimmers and their supporters laughed and clasped their hands to their ears in mock horror at the sound. Mary was encouraged. She had their attention.

'At times like these...' screech '... a song ... rousing ...'

Mary then proceeded to sing 'For those in peril on the sea.' down the megaphone. Mary's voice was weak and tuneless; her choice of song unfortunate; the crowd stood still in amazement at the exhibition. As she was about to launch into the third verse Mr Bennet stepped forward.

'Jolly good Mary. Now let us give someone else a go,' and handed the megaphone to one of the organisers. Mary was disconcerted but cries and hoots of laughter from the crowd diverted her attention. At the far corner of the garden there was a commotion. 'They're coming! They're coming! Make way! Make way!'

The crowds, wolf whistling and shouting encouragement, were parting and moving into the centre to make a track round the edge of the gardens. And round the track were two girls in full flight, screaming, laughing, waving their hands in the air ... and totally naked.

Streakers!

Lizzy stood horrified as the identity of the streakers became apparent. Lydia and Kitty! How could they? As her naked sisters raced past, a whirl of giggling, bouncing femininity, she caught sight of Darcy who had been transfixed by the spectacle in amazement and disbelief. If her family had planned to expose themselves as much as they could that morning they could not have played their parts with more spirit.

Chapter Nineteen

THE following day Mr Collins awoke feeling oysterous. He had been tortured by amorous dreams all night, his passions fuelled by a generous helping of 'oysters au naturel' from the moonlit waterside Oyster Shack restaurant the previous evening and the effect, even by breakfast time was still undeniably strong. Putting mind over matter he considered what Lady Catherine would wish him to do in such a situation and came to the firm belief that she would deem it time for him to make a move in the romantic direction. Anxious for action but unsure how to proceed, the Bennet girls' plan for the day would prove to give him the opportunity he urgently desired. It transpired that they were taking part in the Parachuting Teddies competition from the top of Salcombe church. As fortune would have it Mr Collins had brought his teddy, Malcolm, from whom he had been inseparable from a young age, with him to Salcombe and so, with some misgivings about throwing the said beloved Malcolm from the top of the church tower, attached only to a spotted handkerchief, he felt this was too good an opportunity to miss, and volunteered to take part and accompany the girls.

The weather was bright and breezy. Lasers, toppers and a host of other gaily coloured sailing dinghies scudded about the choppy estuary waters, one or two capsizing as they were caught by mischievous gusts. The sound of loose rigging clanking against masts echoed across the bay and seagulls seemed to squawk louder than normal in their frenetic swooping and diving to feast on dropped croissants crumbs and ice-cream cones. The Bennet girls, Mrs Bennet and Mr Collins set off in the opposite direction from the sea, up the steep hill of Church Street to join the small crowd of people and teddies that were assembling before the church porch of Holy Trinity, Salcombe.

Elizabeth became uncomfortably aware that Mr Collins

was angling to get close to her at every opportunity. He even seemed to make a pretence that his Malcolm wanted to snuggle up to her teddie, Bertie which quite horrified her. Bertie had been her dear companion since earliest childhood and was not to be treated in such a fashion.

The vicar, looking himself like a boat at sea, his white gown flapping relentlessly about his tall, mast-like body, handed out tickets to all teddies and invited owners to make their way in groups up to the top of the tower where their beloved bears, attached to a handkerchief, would be flung out.

'I will time their descent myself,' he added and from deep within his white sail outfit produced a large stopwatch. 'The blessed bear who manages to stay aloft for the longest will be the winner. Off you go and may the Lord be with you and with your teddies!'

The Bennets and Mr Collins were enough to make up Group F and when the time came, set off up the winding stairs. The girls scampered ahead but Mr Collins found his legs would only go at a snail's pace and he was forced to stop on several occasions for a breather. By the time he completed the tortuous climb and stepped out into the open at the top of the turret the girls were already launching their brave teddies into the fresh air. Mrs Bennet, who had made a surprisingly speedy ascent greeted him in a friendly fashion.

'My dear Mr Collins! Well done! Now where is Malcolm? It must be his turn!'

'Malcolm?' Mr Collins looked around. Where indeed was Malcolm? Oh Lord! He must have dropped him on the way up. Mrs Bennet saw an opportunity arise.

'Mr Collins! You must have dropped your teddy on the way up! Poor Malcolm. You rest here and we will look for him on the way down and then one of my girls will run back up with him and you will be able to send him on his way.'

Mrs Bennet had in mind that she would send Lizzy back. It was the perfect opportunity for the two of them to have a tête-à-tête in private. But Mr Collins, the enflamed romantic, was one step ahead!

'Thank you my dear Mrs Bennet. You are most kind. I do find myself rather out of breath, but I would be most grateful if you could ask dear Elizabeth to wait here with me.'

'Of course! Of course!'

'But mama! ...'

'Stay here Lizzy!' hissed Mrs Bennet. 'Come along girls - let's go down at once and see if we can find naughty Malcolm.'

To Lizzy's distress she found herself trapped, alone on top of the tower with Mr Collins. Mr Collins smiled and simpered for a moment and then began.

'My dear Elizabeth. You must know that I ...'

'The view is quite remarkable from here, is it not?' interjected Lizzy, dreading what was to follow. But Mr Collins was not to be put off.

'You must know that I ... that I fancy you. No more! I have the hots for you my dear Elizabeth and with such feelings I am desirous that you will be the companion of my future life.'

Lizzy barely knew whether to laugh or cry but had little chance as Mr Collins was now on a roll.

'My reasons for marrying are one, being a clergyman, I should set an example to my parishioners, two it would make me very happy, three Lady Catherine would be pleased.'

'Wait Mr Collins! You have not given me a chance to respond!'

'Respond! No need for that! I look forward to leading you up the aisle ere long and the well ... all the happiness and the er ...hanky panky that will follow!'

Mr Collins winked and giggled at Lizzy. Lizzy, felt panic rise and her voice rose in parallel.

'No Mr Collins! No!' Her voice trembled in shock and horror which Mr Collins regarded as a passionate response and one which required him to act as befitted an ardent suitor

Down below the vicar and teddy bear parachutists craned

their necks to see what all the hullabaloo at the top of the tower was about. To their horror they could see Lizzy Bennet leaning backwards out over the tower and a strange man leaning over her, throttling her.

It was true Lizzy was in the process of being strangled. Mr Collins was attempting to kiss her, to seal his proposal, but not being familiar with such an act had placed his hands around her neck and as he leant forward, Lizzy leant back in an attempt to escape. The more he pressed the further she leaned until she was in mortal danger of falling out altogether.

'No, Mr Collins! No!'

Later that day Lizzy recoiled with a curious mix of horror, shame and not a little amusement at what happened next. Her situation had been so precarious that she put into action the only weapon known to woman in such a state and kicked out. The effect was instantaneous. Mr Collins let out a howl of agony, let go of her and hurtled across the tower to the other side and to Lizzy's horror flipped over the far edge. She dashed across and peered over expecting to see Mr Collins's mangled body lying far below. Instead she saw his terrified face only a few feet away. By a miracle he had been saved from certain death. His coat had caught on a large hook from which he was now dangling.

'Oh! Oh! Save me! Save me!' he whimpered. 'Oh my! Oh! Oh! Oh!'

The crowd below had run round and were watching in amazement as Lizzy leant through the castellations and managed to pull the unfortunate Mr Collins up until he tottered on the wall and fell back onto the platform crushing Lizzy beneath him.

Chapter Twenty

IT was this sight that met Mrs Bennet and her daughters on their return to the top of the tower.

'Mr Collins!'

Even Mrs Bennet was shocked by the ardour of Lizzy's suitor. She had not expected the clergyman to be so forward in his expression of love as to be already on top of her daughter. How times had changed.

'Madam!' said Mr Collins getting up hastily. 'It is not what it seems! Oh my! Oh my!' and he hurried to the staircase, made his way down as fast as he could, and was surprised as he walked out into the sunshine at the bottom to be hit on the head by a parachuting Malcolm.

'Malcolm had a lovely descent!' called Lydia, giggling from the top of the tower.

'I er ...' Mr Collins left, alone, confused and unsure whether his proposal had been a success of not. He decided to go and sit on a bench and gaze out to sea until the beating in his breast had subsided and he could ask Malcolm for advice.

'Well Lizzy?' asked Mrs Bennet as they descended the winding stairway.

'I will not marry him mother!'

'You certainly will.'

'I shall not.'

'Let's see what your father has to say about this!'

As they left the churchyard they were fortunate enough to bump into Mr Bennet.

'Lizzy will not marry Mr Collins!' announced a furious Mrs Bennet.

'Is this true, Lizzy?'

'I certainly will not!'

'Make her marry him, Mr Bennet! Think of the inheritance.'

'I will not!'

'If you do not, I will never speak to you again!' cried Mrs Bennet.

'Lizzy, my dear,' said Mr Bennet seriously, 'an unhappy situation lies before you. You are on the verge of losing one or other of your parents. If you do not marry Mr Collins your mother will never speak to you again. If you *do* marry Mr Collins, *I* will never speak to you again.'

And with that Mr Bennet walked on leaving Mrs Bennet furious, the Bennet girls in peals of laughter and Lizzy much relieved.

Chapter Twenty One

MR Collins spent the rest of the morning on the wooden bench overlooking pontoons where various holiday boats and fishing vessels were moored and which, fortunately for him was already inhabited by Charlotte Lucas who proved to be a friendly ear. News filtered through by way of passing Bennet girls whispering in Lottie's ear that Lizzy had definitely refused Mr Collins and he sat sulking. When Lizzy, herself, happened to walk by he looked the other way, ignoring her. Lizzy was in fact on the way, with her sisters to North Sands where they were hoping to see some more of the red and yellow trainee lifeguards, and Mr Wickham in particular. As good fortune would have it, Wickham was there and delighted to see Lizzy.

'Sorry I didn't make the Estuary Swim - but you know with Darcy around who knows what might have happened. Best to keep out of shark infested waters!'

There was the evocative sound of Vivaldi's Four Seasons Allegro) from Jane's phone. Jane went over to the rock pools to read the message. Lizzy could tell at once it was not good news and excused herself from the luscious Wickham.

'It is from Cazza.' said Jane. 'Look'

'Hey Jane - jtlyk all off to London 2 party. Not back for yonks. Chas in lve with Darcy's sister, Georgiana ... wedng on way?!! Muchos love Cazza :)'

'The cow!' Lizzy could not help herself. 'She just wants to take Bingley away from you. I could strangle her with her own Boden tights!'

Chapter Twenty Two

CHARLOTTE Lucas's generous ear to Mr Collins had, in Lizzy's mind, a most startling outcome. The two girls had taken the topper out and were enjoying a blustery sail about the estuary when Charlotte felt the moment had come to confide in her best friend.

'Dear Lizzy ...'

'Ready about!' called Lizzy.

'I have some news for you,' continued Lottie as she prepared to go about.

'Lee ho!' shouted Lizzy pushing the tiller hard away from her and swinging the boat into wind and onto a port tack.

'... some news which may surprise you,' continued Lottie as she ducked under the boom.'I am engaged to Mr Collins.'

On this pronouncement of such monstrous news, the topper jibbed alarmingly as Lizzy uncharacteristically los control and both girls were tossed into the sea. The little toppe had turned turtle and as the girls busied themselves righting the craft the extraordinary conversation continued.

'Engaged to Mr Collins?' cried Lizzy astounded. She stoo on the upturned hull and with Lottie's assistance managed t pull the boat so that the mainsail came up and lay flapping o the water. The news was so astonishing to Lizzie and th physical exertion so great that standing on the centreboard an heaving on the side of the boat she could not help crying ou

'Lottie - impossible!'

As she gave true vent to her feelings Lizzy simultaneously pulled with such vehemence that the boat righted itself too fast and went right over onto the other side.

'No I am afraid not,' said Lottie swimming round to help Lizzy pull the boat upright again. 'I see what you are feeling. You must be surprised - only this morning Mr Collins was wishing to marry *you*. But I am not romantic.' Lizzy and Lottie righted the boat at last, toppled in and sat with the sail flapping as Lottie tried to explain to her astonished friend. 'He is not a sensible man, nor agreeable, his society is irksome but all I ask is for a comfortable home; and considering Mr Collins's situation, I am convinced that my chance of happiness with him is as fair, as most people can boast on entering the marriage state.'

'But what about your career? University?'

'My dear Lizzy. My purpose for university would only to be to secure a career or a husband. *Both* are not necessary and indeed, often cancel each other out. Since I already have the husband in hand I have no need for university or career.'

Lizzy was defeated. She pulled at the sheet, set the boat on a starboard tack, smiled as best as she could at her friend and replied kindly,'Undoubtedly, my dear Charlotte.'

As they sailed past The Ferry Inn they saw Mr Collins enjoying a Bloody Mary. He smiled at Lottie and blew her a kiss, only briefly glancing, with a triumphant smirk at Lizzy. How sweet was a jilted lovers revenge!

Chapter Twenty Three

Sir William Lucas was triumphant in Lottie's engagement. Mrs Bennet was furious. Lady Lucas enjoyed her visits to 3 Island Street all the more, since in time her daughter would inherit it. Mr Collins - the cause of all the upset - departed for Rosings to tell Lady Catherine the good news.

Chapter Twenty Four

'HEY Jane. - jtlyk having g8 time in London. Chas and Georgina v close! Wedng bells rngng! Muchos love Cazza :)'

'Yo gals! Why the miserable faces?'

The jolly smile of Wickham revived the spirits of Jane and Lizzy as they sat dangling their legs over the quayside, trying to catch crabs with bits of bacon strung to fishing lines, whilst pondering this latest evil missive from Cazza Bingley. Jane was still determined to think well of her, Lizzy could only think ill and was sure Chas was still as crazy as ever about her sister. But it was strange, she must confess for Bingley to have left so suddenly and without even saying goodbye.

'Caught one!' cried Lizzy, diverted by an encrusted crab that had just grabbed hold of her bait. Wickham gallantly attempted to remove the crustacean from her hook but in doing so was pinched viciously.

'Why! It's a damn Darcy of a crab!' he cried letting go. And so the conversation turned to Mr Darcy, what an appalling cad he was and how nobody, apart from Jane who could criticise nobody, had a good word to say about him. In short, he was universally despised.

Chapter Twenty Five

MRS Bennet's misery was soon to be diverted by the arrival of her brother, Mr Gardiner, his wife, Mrs Gardiner and a lively bunch of nephews and nieces. Aunt G was a great favourite of Jane and Lizzy and despite their mothers complaining how both had been nearly married or at least had a boyfriend and now neither were and neither had even a boyfriend, they managed to escape from time to time for a session at the lively Fortescue, where over a bottle of blush and a game of poo they talked of university options. After the merits of Durham, Bristol, Exeter, York, St Andrews, Oxford, King's College, London, Edinburgh, Plymouth, Bath and Brighton had been discussed at length, the last ball potted and Jane had left, temporarily, to wash her hands, the talk turned to love.

'But Bingley is completely and utterly crazy about her Aunt G!' said Lizzy sitting down at a small wooden table and drawing up another stool for her aunt. Lizzy was anxious for her wise aunt to understand the situation clearly.

'Many a young man declares himself crazy about a pretty girl one week and then another the next,' demurred Aunt G.

'Yes but this is the real thing,' insisted Lizzy leaning forward. 'He is insanely in love. Anyone could see that. He hangs on Jane's every word, follows her around like a devoted spaniel, ignores all the other Salcombe babes.'

'So why has he abandoned her?'

'Because his sister and the despicable Darcy think she is not good enough for him. They have stolen Bingley away!'

Aunt G gasped at this revelation, recovering only just in time to welcome Jane back to the table where the evening took a very merry turn as they were joined by the jovial Wickham. Another bottle of blush led to some jolly banter. Aunt G could not fail to notice the glow that passed between Lizzy and Wickham. Common ground in knowledge of the late Mr Darcy was found between Wickham and Aunt G which led to much discourse about Darcy's father - a fine old gentleman both agreed - and of his proud, ill-natured boy of whose characteristics Wickham was quite clear and Aunt G had to search her memory banks to see if she could recall what the boy was like, but was guided by Wickham until at last she did vaguely recall that he might have been proud and ill-natured. Last orders were called and the four returned in a slightly unsteady state to 3 Island Street for coffee where lively conversation continued until the early hours.

Chapter Twenty Six

Mr Collins returned. He had the blessing of Lady Catherine de Brrr to marry and was keen to get on with things. Although there had already been four weddings and a funeral at Salcombe church that week, the vicar, once assured by Sir William Lucas that all the correct proceedures had been completed, agreed to squeeze in one more wedding for Mr Collins and his fiancée. After the ceremony the glowing groom whisked his young bride away to Hunsford. Throughout the whole affair Lizzy tried to be happy for her friend but she actually felt sick. How could Lottie have sacrificed herself in such a way? Still, they promised to text regularly, though Lizzy felt the intimacy had gone out of the relationship with such a barrier as Mr Collins between them.

Meanwhile, romance for the Bennet girls was seriously on the slide. Jane had buzzed off to London with Aunt G and Uncle G. She had called in on Cazza who was courteous but cool and said Chas was busy with Darcy. Poor Jane was under no illusion that she had been dumped. Lizzy meanwhile noticed Wickham's attentions had moved on too, to Mary King, a young lady who had just inherited a pink hulled speedboat. Lizzy's fortunes were no match for this. Like her dear sister, she too had been dumped.

Chapter Twenty Seven

YET startling news was to follow. Lady Catherine had condescended to offer the lodge of her magnificent Salcombe holiday home, 'Rosings on the Rocks', to the newly wed Mr and Mrs Collins as a honeymoon holiday destination Lottie and Mr Collins would be returning to Salcombe to stay in 'Little Rosings on the Rocks' and Lady Catherine hersel would be installed in the main house. Lizzy, Sir William and Maria Lucas had been invited to stay for a few days at Little Rosings. Lady Catherine felt it would do them good to get out of the damp lowlands of Island Street, into the uplands of Cliff Road, and besides she wanted to inspect them.

Chapter Twenty Eight

LIZZY packed her blue and white Quba bag and set off in Angelica with Sir William, Lady Lucas and Maria, Lottie's sweet but dim sister. Mr Bennet came with them so they could disembark on Rosings on the Rocks' private jetty and he could return in the boat. Sir William kept a constant flow of conversation going during the voyage but fortunately his words were swept away by the breeze or drowned out by Maria's squawks every time water splashed over the bows. After landing they waved farewell to Mr Bennet and started the trudge up the steep rocky path to Little Rosings on the Rocks - only a short distance but by the time they arrived Sir William was sweating profusely. Standing before the little lodge house were the honeymoon couple, suitable dressed in swimwear - Mr Collins bucking the Salcombe trend for swim shorts was clad in skimpy Speedos and Lottie looked attractive in a delightful stripy all in one from Crew. Suddenly Mr Collins caught sight of something, or someone and ran helter skelter down towards their private jetty. A sleek black Phantom speedboat appeared from nowhere and skidded to a stop at the jetty, drenching him in spray from head to toe. A small exchange between the driver and Mr Collins occurred and the boat sped off again. Mr Collins turned beaming to welcome his guests and to announce with great delight the marvellous news. Lady Catherine had condescended to invite them all to Rosings on the Rocks for dinner that very night.

Chapter Twenty Nine

POOR Maria was in a state of great anxiety as she rummaged through her kit bag desperately trying to find something suitable to wear for the evening's entertainment. Lizzy was pleased with her recent Jack Wills purchases: an Elsie Cotton Shirt, pink and white striped which she wore with the sleeves turned up; a 100% cotton Fonshaw Mini Fit antique denim skirt which sat low on her hips; the Donnell Leather Belt. Mr Collins was happy that she looked if anything a little relaxed for the occasion as it was important not to out-dazzle Lady Catherine.

Rosings on the Rocks was everything Mr Collins had boasted. Set in a concrete frame with steel bracing it had an excess of glass curtain walling with unrivalled views of the estuary.

'The structure,' explained Mr Collins, 'is expressed as an ornamental order, the style high-tech modern. It has an unapologetic modern facade, combining a jagged profile in an elegant concrete frame that is braced by gunmetal gray and stainless steel rods oozing an airy spirit full of honesty but not lacking in bravado.'

Lizzy was amazed by Mr Collins erudite description and for one horrible moment thought she might have misjudged him but Lottie soon explained: 'A speech he has practised for sometime,' she whispered. 'Architecture Week magazine. Different building but surprisingly appropriate.'

At that moment a tall, powerful woman appeared on the balcony. She was dressed in skintight black jeans, a black strappy top embroidered with 'Brrr' in diamante. Her dyed blond hair was piled high, her nails painted blood red, her feet adorned with high heeled golden slippers.

'Collywobbles dahling!' she called. 'Here you are at last and with all your little friends. Come on in! The Blood Mary's are waiting!'

Lady Catherine condescended to kiss each and every one of her guests on each cheek - twice as Mr Collins recalled.

'Now you must be little Maria,' she cooed. 'What a babe! Lottie dahling - you never told me your little sis was so cute!' and she went on in this vein welcoming all her guests to the delight of Mr Collins.

'Now Collywobbles - who is this?'

'Miss Elizabeth Bennet.'

'And how old are you, Miss Elizabeth Bennet?'

'You surely would not expect a lady to reveal her age, madam,' replied Lizzy.

'Oh! Quite a feisty number I see' retorted Lady Catherine, maintaining her good humour even if she did feel put out by Lizzy's reply. 'Come on. Let's eat. We have lobster tonight. I have my own pot of course. Does your family have a pot Miss Elizabeth Bennet?'

'No I am afraid we do not have a pot. And please do call me Lizzy.'

'Not a pot! I pity you Miss Elizabeth Bennet!'

At that moment Lizzy noticed a rather large, overweight girl lazing around on a leather poof. To her surprise she was introduced as Miss De Brrr. Her eyes were fixed on her Wii and she failed to join in conversation once all evening. Lizzy smiled to herself. She felt Miss De Brrr would indeed make the perfect partner for a certain gentleman.

Mr Collins was in his element admiring the view, the golden statues of King Charles spaniels with their diamante collars, the Maria Theresa chandelier, the abstract paintings by Gotspod and being quite overcome - and off balanced - by the black and chrome revolving stools that they sat on to eat cracked lobster from a high chrome and blackened glass table.

'It's all bullet proof, of course' pronounced Lady Catherine as Mr Collins admired the glass curtain for the umpteenth time.

'And I always wear a bullet proof vest,' she continued. 'In my position you can never be too careful. Do you wear a bullet proof vest, Miss Elizabeth Bennet?'

'Rarely.'

'That is very foolish.'

'I find it hard to accommodate under a bikini. Do you wear a bikini Lady Catherine?'

The boldness of this remark made other members of the party draw a sharp intake of breath.

'You are a bold and foolish girl, Miss Elizabeth Bennet but I will excuse you this once as you clearly are new to such company as occurs at Rosings on the Rocks.'

An awkward silence followed broken only by Maria getting a small amount of shell stuck in her throat. She began to cough and then choke. She fell from her rotating stool and lay on the white carpet, spluttering and gasping for breath.

'She is choking,' remarked Lady Catherine.

'It must be a bit of shell stuck in her throat!' exclaimed Lizzy in great anxiety and leaping off her stool to assist.

'It could not be shell.' declared Lady Catherine. 'Our lobsters never have shell that would make you choke. It must be something else. Perhaps one of those cheap baubles she is wearing round her neck has come loose and she has swallowed one. Yes. That is what is making her choke. Believe me. I am always right in these matters.'

By this stage Maria was unable to speak and had stopped coughing and more alarmingly stopped breathing. Lizzy proceeded to carry out the Heimlich manoeuvre by giving her five subdiaphragmatic abdominal thrusts alternating with five back blows to remove the obstruction whilst the others continued with their cracked lobster, and discussing what Maria might or might not have swallowed with Lady Catherine continuing a powerful argument why it could not be one of her lobsters at fault. As Maria slipped into unconsciousness Lizzy turned her on her back, requested a 999 call - though nobody heard - and placing the heel of her hand just above Maria's waistline proceeded to give four upward thrusts. Lady Catherine was just saying, yet again how her lobsters could not have caused such a problem - in fact they were renowned for being the safest lobsters in the estuary - when there was a horrible gurgling sound from Maria and a cough that seemed to come from her very soul. A hard brittle object shot out of her mouth and landed with a tinkle on Lady Catherine's plate. It was quite clearly a piece of lobster shell.

'You see!' cried Lady Catherine in triumph. 'I was right. It *is* lobster shell but not from one of *my* lobsters! You must have had a lobster sandwich for lunch Maria and a bit of shell got lodged in your teeth and you just happened to swallow it while you were eating *my* lobster!'

Lady Catherine pincered the offending shell between two sharp red nails and held it aloft for closer inspection.

'Most definitely *not* one of my lobsters! I knew I was right. I always am in such matters. Now who would like some Rosings on the Rocks ice-cream for pudding. We have quite the best ice-cream you will have ever tasted. It is made for me by Ollie James, a chef of great repute, who heard me discussing my ice-cream one day and was so impressed he begged me for the recipe and now sells it by the boatload.'

By this stage Maria had regained consciousness and Lizzy was advising her to rest. But Maria, though a frightened rabbit by nature, was also very fond of ice-cream and recovered sufficiently to join the party for pudding.

Thus a successful evening was rounded off with much thanks from Mr Collins and his party and an announcement by Lady Catherine on what the weather would be on the morrow.

Chapter Thirty

THE following day, Sir William, confident that his daughter was in good hands and happily married, returned to his own abode. Lizzy now spent her time swimming from the private bay, snorkling and fishing off the rocks. Mr Collins spent his time dashing up to Rosings on the Rocks whenever he was summoned and Lottie spent her time between the two. Another great excitement was in store for Mr Collins. He had been told by Lady Catherine that Mr Darcy was expected at the main house and sure enough, that afternoon the good ship Pemberley could be seen gliding into the harbour and minutes later it's tender, a fine wooden rowing boat with 12hp engine came into view, bringing with it two gentlemen. The first to disembark on the private jetty was Colin Fitzwilliam, a cousin of Darcy's - not a handsome man but so well fitted out in a fabulously British Jack Wills blazer and so amiable that he was clearly a gentleman. Darcy equally well dressed was as reserved as ever. As the group gathered on the jetty he said nothing until, for the sake of civility enquired after Lizzy's family.

'Are your family as barmy as ever madam?' he enquired all politeness.

'Yes. Quite as barmy,' Lizzy replied, 'apart from Jane of course. She has been in London. Did you not happen to see her.'

Darcy blanched, and nearly lost his footing on the lichen covered jetty. Moments later the gentlemen departed for the main house.

Chapter Thirty One

AFTER luncheon Mr Collins received an invitation to join his patroness at the Sandcastle Competition. The invitation was by text: 'Collywobbles. The Sandcastle Competition takes place this afternoon at South Sands. My artistic superiority would be missed if I did not take part. Join us. LCdB.'

'Oh my! Oh my! The annual Sandcastle Competition. Oh lord. What shall I do? You must all think of a subject. We must not disgrace ourselves in front of Lady Catherine. Oh my! Oh my! She is coming! We must hurry!'

Mr Collins raced round gathering buckets, spades and his favourite little rake for making marks on the sand and was only stopped in his hunt for any other vital equipment by the appearance of Lady Catherine herself in the doorway.

'You all know the rules I presume?' said Lady Catherine and without waiting for any response continued, 'we may work in small groups to portray either a traditional sandcastle or a humourous sandcastle. The best wins. You can make sandcastles to a high standard I presume Miss Elizabeth Bennet?'

'To a moderate standard.'

'Then you will learn from me. Come along Darcy!'

With that she swept away and started the walk to South Sands her arm linked firmly with Darcy's whose other arm was struggling to hold all the buckets and spades that Lady Catherine had insisted *he* carrried.

Lizzy found herself in the fortunate position of falling into step with Colin who made the most amiable of conversation. Their laughter caused not only Lady Catherine to turn round from time to time to enquire what was so funny and that she must be alerted to it for there was no doubt she would find whatever was so funny funnier than anyone as she had a very fine sense of humour and found anything funny very funny indeed, but also caused Darcy to turn round and look at the couple with curiosity.

After trawling up Cliff Road, down to North Sands and up again, over the pine cladded cliffs, the party made the final descent to South Sands. Through the trees they could already see a hundred or so families and little groups preparing their area on the beach, ready for the start of the competition.

'Hurry!' commanded Lady Catherine and the little party hurried down onto the beach. On arrival Darcy managed to identify a good patch of sand not yet claimed.

'I will create a magnificent traditional sandcastle here with Miss De Brrr,' announced Lady Catherine. 'You, Miss Elizabeth Bennet, will enter the humourous category since you find life so amusing. You may dig there.'

With her pink spade she pointed to a shingly patch.

'The rest of you may join whichever group you prefer although I daresay you will learn somewhat more from watching *my* sandcastle skills.'

Mr Collins advised Lottie that they would be best to take advantage of Lady Catherine's condescending offer and went to join her. To Lizzy's delight Colin came to join her, and to her surprise - and Lady Catherine's irritation - so did Darcy.

'Mr Darcy! I am surprised,' Lizzy owned honestly 'I did not think humour was something you would seek out?'

'Rarely it is true. But I can enjoy a joke from time to time. Did you hear the one about the ...'

At that moment the hooter went for the competition to start. All around groups fell into immediate action, like lots of rabbits, scooping out, burrowing down, sending sand flying building sand up, hunting for pebbles and seaweed for decoration.

To Mr Collins's surprise Lady Catherine produced a deckchair from nowhere, sat down, told him to take off his shoes, roll up his trousers and get to work. With the help of Lottie he was soon digging until his heart would burst, a great mound of sand, required before any skillful artistry would be needed.

Lizzy's team were, it has to be said, caught out by the hooter.

'Let us start to dig at least, while we try to think of an idea,' suggested Colin.

Darcy grabbed a small red spade and set too with a vengeance. The sun was up and his vigorous activity meant he soon felt the heat. He had sometime ago removed socks and shoes, and now removed his shirt revealing a muscular torso and leaving him only in his shorts. Still he worked on.

Lizzy had let her hair loose and had stripped down to her bikini top, although, for modesty's sake had kept her shorts on. She looked, in Darcy's opinion, just like a mermaid - and he made the error of murmuring his thoughts aloud.

'A mermaid?' repeated Colin loudly. 'A mermaid is a good idea Darcy,' he continued mistaking Darcy's train of thought, 'but hardly humourous.'

'Unless,' Lizzy chipped in with a mischievous twinkle in her eye, 'unless the mermaid were a man! You enjoy a joke Mr Darcy. You said so yourself but a minute ago. Why don't *you* lie down and we can cover you to the waist in all this sand and shape it into a tail, then make a bikini top for you out of shells and you would look divine with long seaweed hair.'

'I don't think ...'

'Stop protesting Darcy! Lizzy's idea is a splendid one. Come on! Lie down!' insisted Colin, delighted.

Before he knew it, Darcy was lying down on the sand and despite his initial misgivings began to enjoy unexpected benefits.

'I fear my fingers do not move in the masterly manner which I see so many women's do,' said Elizabeth as she piled up and patted sand over Darcy's taut lower stomach and down his firm thighs towards his toes in an attempt to make a mermaid tail. 'They have not the same force or rapidity, and do not produce the same expression. But then I have always supposed it to be my own fault - because I would not take the trouble of practising.'

Darcy who was finding the experience alarmingly satisfying smiled and said, 'You are perfectly right. You have employed your time much better. Although,' he added, 'I feel you have a natural ability and sensitivity in such matters which may belie your lack of experience.'

They were interrupted by Lady Catherine calling out to see what they were talking of. Lizzy immediately got to work collecting shells for the mermaid's top to avoid further conversation while Colin busied himself searching for long trails of seaweed to make lovely waves of floating hair. The shells and seaweed found, Darcy lay in perfect contentment as Colin spent time at the tail end making fish like indentations and Lizzy busied herself arranging the shells on his chest and the seaweed around his face until he looked as delightful as he felt.

During this time Lady Catherine had been giving artistic direction to Mr Collins and Lottie as they endeavoured to build a sandcastle in the shape of Rosings which Lady Catherine knew would win the hearts of the judges. It was a challenging task, as Rosings lacked the turrets which generally so clearly identify a traditional sandcastle. Miss De Brrr was forced to sit through it all, looking white and pale, under the shade of an umbrella, feeling too ill to contribute which had she been able to - as Lady Catherine later commented - would have been a great help as Miss De Brrr would probably be one of the finest traditional sandcastle makers in the country if she had ever had the chance to learn. As it was, when the final hooter went, Mr Collins' efforts looked merely like a pile of sand rather than a castle and the judges passed their effort without awarding any prizes. Lady Catherine was frozen in fury. It took her five minutes to recover her good humour whereupon she enquired,'Where is Darcy?'

Her good humour was to disappear again for several hours on finding Darcy.

'Over here!' came the voice of her nephew and there to her horror she saw him. Darcy was lying on the sand, a beautiful mermaid's tail covering him from the waist down, his fine chest adorned in a skimpy shell top, and long flowing seaweed hair surrounding his handsome face. Worse still he was smiling and looking quite content. Even worse he was gazing adoringly at Miss Elizabeth Bennet. And to cap it all, gently placed above his ear, in a most becoming manner, was a red rosette. First Prize. It was all too much. Lady Catherine stormed off leaving Mr Collins to carry her buckets, spades, deck chairs, umbrellas and Miss De Brrr, who would have walked herself so beautifully if she ever had been in the habit of walking for herself.

Chapter Thirty Two

THE following day Mr Collins, Lottie and Maria had set off by boat to Kingsbridge to purchase some items so Lizzy took the chance to pop down to the small ribbon of sand below Rosings on the Rocks to read her latest blockbuster and to text Jane. She had just started her novel, which, even though alone, made her blush by the racy contents of it's opening chapter, when she was startled to see a figure jump down the rocks onto the beach, making no use of the steps, and was more startled to see that that figure was Mr Darcy. He seemed, too, astonished at finding her alone and although he apologised for disturbing her did not leave. Instead he spread out his multi-coloured beach towel besides her and sat down staring at the sea.

Lizzy was perplexed. She tried to continue to read but found it impossible with him sitting so close and besides, the contents of her book were making her uncomfortable. She must speak.

'How suddenly you left Salcombe earlier Mr Darcy! I trust Bingley is enjoying himself still in London? '

'Yes.'

'And does he have any plans to return to Netherpollock?'

'It is unlikely.'

At that moment the Kingsbridge party returned and Lottie and Maria made their way to the beach. They were much surprised to see Lizzy and Darcy there alone and Darcy made haste to leave.

'Lizzy! What is the meaning of this?' cried Charlotte as soon as he was gone.

'He loves ya! He loves ya!' chanted Maria who only stopped when Lizzy, laughing and denying any such thing, picked up the screaming Maria and dumped her in the sea.

Chapter Thirty Three

IT seemed strange to Lizzy that in her ramblings over the next few days Darcy always seemed to pop up by some remarkable coincidence: while drinking Pinot Grigio with Lottie in the secret garden of the Victoria Inn he was sitting at the next table nursing a Bells; walking over to Bolt Head he appeared in a gorse bush; on a cliff side walk to the Pig's Nose Inn at East Prawle she was followed not only by Parsnip, the inn's friendly little dog, but also by Darcy; fishing out by Hope Cove he happened to swim by; even scrambling over the rocks at Mill Bay he seemed busy with his net in the very next rock pool.

On one occasion however, it was Colin that Lizzy happened upon when skimming out at The Bar, the stretch of sand at the mouth of the estuary, only exposed at low tide at which time it becomes a great favourite with those who like to skim along the wet surface on their surfboards. Lizzy, looking most athletic in her wetsuit, happened to pass Colin as he whizzed in the opposite direction. They stopped for a chat which soon turned to the topic of Mr Darcy and his sister Georgiana. Lizzy did not wish the opportunity to pass without gleaning a little more information on behalf of Jane.

'I have heard only good things of Georgiana. She is a favourite of Caroline Bingley I understand.'

'Yes. Her brother is good mates with Darcy.'

'Oh yes! Darcy is good mates with Bingley and takes great care of him.'

'You are right there. I do believe Darcy does take care of Bingley. Why! I have heard that Darcy managed to save Bingley from a most disastrous marriage. Apparently he nearly married into a ghastly family. The girl had the most hideous mother and outrageous sisters. Near escape so they say. Cheers.' And with that Colin skimmed away, unwittingly leaving Lizzy in a state of great anxiety, her heart bursting in fury against the detestable Darcy.

Chapter Thirty Four

MOMENTS later another figure in black skimmed towards her. To her horror it was the detestable Darcy himself. He skidded to a halt before her, his taut, muscular body trapped within a black rubbery wetsuit and with a strange, manic look in his eye stared at her for a full two minutes before speaking whereupon he blurted out,

'It's no good Lizzy. I love you deeply and desperately.'

Now it was Lizzy's turn to stare back with a strange, manic look in her eye. He went on.

'I realise your family is odious, you mother quite hideous and your sisters outrageous but for some nonsensical reason I can't help loving you deeply and desperately. What do you have to say?'

Lizzy's astonishment was beyond expression. Despite her dislike of Darcy, she could not help to be a little flattered by such attentions. But then her anger rose.

He had made it quite clear that he liked her against his

better judgement. Was this a compliment or an insult she challenged.

'But even if *my* feelings had been favourable to you,' she continued, growing in fury, ' do you think I could be tempted by the man who has ruined the happiness of a beloved sister, perhaps for ever? And what is more you have reduced another, Mr Wickham, to comparative poverty, withheld advantages designed for him and deprived him of independence which was his due.'

Darcy grew pale.

'And this is your opinion of me?'

'I have no qualms in expressing my opinion. You have saved me the concern I might have felt in refusing you, if you had behaved in a more gentleman-like manner.'

Lizzy saw Darcy start at this and feeling there was little more to be said took the only course available to her and slapped him across the face. He fell backwards into the water and Lizzy, not knowing what to do next, skimmed away as fast as she possibly could.

Chapter Thirty Five

AN hour later Lizzy, now back at Little Rosings on the Rocks found herself restless and unable to settle at any useful occupation. Her surprise at what had just passed could not be greater. Her heart and soul were in turmoil so she resolved to indulge in air and exercise. Slipping the wooden sailing dinghy that came with Rosings on the Rocks from it's mooring, she hoisted the white mainsail and jib and set sail for the open seas.

The breeze was strong and white horses broke threateningly over the top of the waves as she left the safety of the estuary. But Lizzy was in no mood to be cautious. The more the spray threw itself over the bows the more reckless she felt. Feelings of fury, insult and humiliation lashed her as cruelly as the bite of the wind. It was only as she passed Prawle Point she became aware of another sailing boat coming up fast to her starboard. It cut suddenly across her bows.

'Hey you idiot!' yelled Lizzy when to her surprise the boat tacked and drew up alongside her. It was Darcy!

'Miss Elizabeth!' he called.

Lizzy was furious and jibbed to escape him. It was a dangerous move and she nearly capsized but righting the boat just in time found he had tacked and was sailing along her port side, whereupon he handed her a bottle, with a screw top, within which was a letter.

'Miss Elizabeth,' he shouted above the wind and the waves. 'I have been sailing back and forth around Prawle Point some time in the hope of meeting you. Will you do me the honour of reading that letter?'

And with a slight bow Darcy himself jibbed and was soon out of sight.

With no expectation of pleasure but with the strongest curiosity Lizzy turned into wind and allowed the sails to flap wildly whilst she tried to extricate the said letter from the bottle. It was not an easy task as the sea was choppy and she was constantly rocked from side to side but Lizzy persisted and at last she had the letter freed and in her hand. Spray caused the ink to splodge in many places but huddling over and constantly wiping water away she endeavoured to read through the two sheets of letter paper written quite through, in a very close hand.

'Be not alarmed, Madam, on receiving this letter.'

Lizzy *was* alarmed and being alone at sea found herself reading out loud those phrases that struck her most:

'I will not repeat my sentiments which were so disgusting to you. I write only to clarify the the two offences you laid to my charge. Yes Bingley was in love with your sister but from my observations I did not think *she* reciprocated and this combined with the ghastly behaviour of certain members of your family - sorry to offend you - encouraged me as a friend to discourage my friend. There is but one part of my conduct in the whole affair on which I do not reflect with satisfaction - I did conceal from Bingley your sister's presence in town. If I have wounded your sister's feelings, it was unknowingly done. As for Wickham ...'

A sudden spray made much of what followed illegible but enough remained for Lizzy to understand the heinous behaviour of that young gentleman. Wickham had wasted money and opportunity bestowed upon him by Darcy's generous father. When this source of money had dried up he planned to elope with Georgiana, Darcy's sister, his object being the young girl's fortune! But at the last minute Georgiana confessed the plan to her brother, whom she looked up to as a father and Darcy foiled the elopement, saving his sister from disaster and writing to Wickham who, seeing the game was up, left immediately!

So Wickham wanted revenge on Darcy! All along he had tainted Darcy's character in her eyes - in the eyes of al Salcombe society!

The final words of Darcy's now soggy letter swam before her eyes.

'I will only add, God bless you.

Fitzwilliam Darcy'.

Chapter Thirty Six

OH! Oh! Oh! Lizzy scarcely knew what to think. She pulled i the mainsheet as if to gather her thoughts but jibbed instantl then almost immediately went about in error and was i danger of being thrown into the waters. The little boat rocke and rolled on the tempestuous seas. She began with prejudice against his every word. How could he pretend that he was insensible to Jane's feelings? That must be false! How could he find her family such an objection? And where was the apology? Only a hint of wrongdoing at concealing Jane's existence in London. But hardly an apology. Yes he was all pride and insolence.

Lizzy went about putting the boat onto a starboard tack, heading straight out to sea. She was in no mood to return. What mood she was in she hardly knew. The sun came out and glinted over the breaking waves. The dark clouds became rimmed with silver and the little boat struck forth intrepidly through the waters. But where Lizzy's mind was going she could not say. After her fury but confirmation of feelings at the first part of the letter she found the account of Wickham filled her with astonishment, apprehension, even horror. She thought back of her times with Wickham and blushed at her own forwardness, her own fondness, his impropriety - yes impropriety - at discussing Darcy's faults so freely with her aunt - then a stranger to him. Oh! And what of Mary King? Of course, the pink hulled speedboat. Despite the cold wind Lizzy felt herself redden at the thought of any affection she had had with Wickham. She had been well and truly duped.

But what then of Darcy? Perhaps ... she re-read the letter again. Charlotte's words rang in her ears that Jane should not be too secretive about her affections. How she had teased her friend then but perhaps after all Lottie had been right. Jane *was* in danger of loosing the man she loved by disguising her feelings too well. As for the comments about her family - she blushed at the outrageous behaviour at the Estuary Swim. It was a ghastly exhibition. Her mind rambled on over the events of the summer since first meeting Darcy and Bingley. Each memory of each encounter caused her excruciating embarrassment and an immediate wish to expunge all recollection of her behaviour towards Darcy. Physical exertion seemed her only immediate escape. She pulled in the jib, jamming its sheet into its clamp, and heaved in the mainsheet as tight as possible, forcing the boat to keel over and pushing herself out on the gunnels, leaning right back over the waters to prevent capsizing. In this manner she battled fiercely with the waves, the wind and her feelings until she felt able to return to Little Rosings on the Rocks and appear cheerful as usual.

On her return, soaking and exhausted, she was told that earlier Darcy had called for a few moments, apparently soaked and exhausted, then left. Sometime later Colin had called and waited and waited for her and eventually with a sigh had also left. Lizzy could only pretend to affect concern at missing him; she really rejoiced. Colin was no longer an object. She could think only of her letter.

Chapter Thirty Seven

DARCY and Colin had left Rosings on the Rocks that afternoon and Lizzy decided to leave Little Rosings shortly after. She had a call from Mr Bennet begging her to return. With Jane also away he was finding no moment of sense with the rest of the family and fearing for his own sanity could do with her company.

Chapter Thirty Eight

AT lunchtime Lizzy, taking Maria with her, said her goodbye to dear Lottie and thanked Mr Collins (who laboured over their leaving a great deal and without necessity) and returned by water taxi and with much relief to 3 Island Street.

Chapter Thirty Nine

As the water taxi glided past The Ferry Inn Lizzy's attention was caught by screams and turning her head towards the shore saw Kitty and Lydia leaning over The Ferry Inn wall waving wildly at them. Lizzy waved back and instructed the taxi to drop her off at the Inn were she and Maria went and joined her sisters in the stone garden. Kitty and Lydia were in high spirits. On the table was a spread of mussels, oysters and crab for the girls to enjoy as a reunion lunch.

'Is it not kind of us?' said Kitty.

'And we mean to treat you,' added Lydia, 'only you will have to lend us the money as we have just spent all ours in Amelia's Attic on this gorgeous clippy art bag and this sun hut from Joules. I don't really like the hat though but I thought I might as well buy it as not.'

'And guess what the big news is Lizzy?' said Kitty.

'Mary King has given Wickham the boot!' interrupted Lydia stealing Kitty's thunder. 'What do you think of that Lizzy? Are you thrilled?'

'I just think Mary King has had a lucky escape,' said Lizzy smiling.

'Who cares about Mary King anyway? I'm starving. Let's start!'

The girls had a very merry lunch and walked back down Fore Street arm in arm and singing jollily until they reached 3 Island Street where Mary was sitting studying Advanced Physics and whose only greeting on seeing Lizzy was 'Shhhh'.

Chapter Forty

LATER as Lizzy and Jane sat crabbing on Victoria Quay Jane squeaked in surprise at news of Darcy's attentions to Lizzy. Lizzy calmed her but she squeaked again on hearing what a bad egg Wickham had been. She could never have thought one human being could be quite so ghastly!

Chapter Forty One

THERE was a scream from 3 Island Street to disturb the girls' intimate deep meaningful conversation. Seconds later Lydia came rushing down Victoria Quay, her face beaming, her eyes alight with excitement. Mrs Forster whose husband, Colonel Foster, trained all the lifeguards, had invited her to join them at the official lifeguard summer camp at South Sands!

'I'm off to stay at South Sands,' she yelled in rapturous delight. Kitty came trawling behind her crying 'It's not fair! It's so like not fair!'

Lizzy was horrified. Goodness knows what mischief Lydia would get up to, running riot amongst all the red and yellows. 'Father!' she implored, 'Lydia will embarrass the whole family and cause untold damage!'

'Poor Lizzy!' replied Mr Bennet. 'Has your naughty little sister been upsetting your lovers. Tut! Tut! I say the further away she is from here the better.'

'It's not fair! It's so like not fair!' cried Kitty.

Wickham, who would of course be returning to South Sands for hard lifeguard training came to say 'hello' and 'cheerio' to Lizzy. He could not help probing her for a little info: 'Were there any other guests while you were at Little Rosings on the Rocks?'

'We had the pleasure of Mr Darcy and the delightful Coli

staying at Rosings on the Rocks both of whom we saw a great deal and both of whom appeared only the more delightful the more one saw of them and learnt of their true natures and histories.'

'I ... oh ... um ... well cherio then,' said Wickham in confusion and he left, tripping only over his own feet, so as to tumble out head first into Island Street.

Chapter Forty Two

LYDIA away, Kitty in constant tears about *not* being away, Mary with her eyes glazed and nose in a book and Jane bravely trying not to be upset, Lizzy was grateful to be invited on a trip north with her uncle and aunt, during which they planned to visit Durham University. The day came for her to leave and Mr Bennet took her up the estuary in Angelica to Kingsbridge where she would catch the Tally Ho bus to Totnes and thereafter, having breakfasted in the splendid greasy spoon station café, take the train up to Durham, where she would meet her uncle and aunt.

Lizzy had considered all universities with care and had still to be tempted north but Aunt G's glowing reports about Durham and in particular University College which was situated in the world heritage status Durham Castle had aroused her curiosity.

'The students actually live in the castle,' Aunt G had enthused. 'And what a castle! No other college in the British Isles could have a more ancient or impressive home! 900 years old and placed high on the Bailey with Durham Cathedral just across Palace Green and almost totally surrounded by the River Wear. And as for the little cobbled streets and ancient buildings my dear, you will be enchanted.'

The journey north was long but pleasantly spent in completing her racy blockbuster, texting old pals, listening to

Duffy on her ipod and dozing and before she knew it Lizzy was opening the door of her carriage and throwing herself into the arms of her uncle and aunt as they waited excitedly on Durham station. Without further ado they set off for the castle.

Chapter Forty Three

WHEN at last the massive structure of Durham Castle reared into view Lizzy's spirits were in a flutter. It's great stone turrets rose high above the small city, only rivalling in height the spires of the adjacent medieval cathedral. The trio walked across Elvet Bridge and turned left into Saddler Street. Lizzy was glad of her stout shoes for the cobbled streets could undoubtedly cause a twist to anyone in high heels. They turned up the Georgian passage of Owengate and there before them, rising dramatically to the right was Durham Castle, the flat, beautifully mown Palace Green before them and Durham Cathedral to their left. Lizzy hardly knew which way to look.

'Now my dear,' explained Aunt G, 'the students of course have not yet returned for term but I understand that if we ask at the gatehouse the porter might show us round the castle itself.'

'Oh I do hope so!' breathed Lizzy, captivated.

The little party walked down the cobbled entrance to the castle where they enquired at the ancient gatehouse whether it would be possible to have a tour. The porter was a delightful gentleman who explained that normally students would take tours for prospective students, such a prospective student he presumed the lovely young lassie before him to be, but since the regular students were off on their holidays traipsing round Vietnam and Goa and such places, enjoying themselves catching malaria, scabies, leprosy and the like, he would have the great pleasure of taking the tour himself. With that he got out a massive key that swung from a great belt round his girth locked the gatehouse and invited the party to follow him. The porter, who introduced himself as 'Reynolds', was a mine of information and an overflowing pot of enthusiasm for the place. 'Howay man, I'll show you round with pleasure,' he promised and led them down to the ancient Tunstall Chapel.

'1540 this was built, pet. These days it's packed out down here at Christmas, all lit by candles, a comforting gloom and then the singing starts! Enough to raise the spirits of the dead by its beauty it is! Oh that it is!'

Reynolds then led them up the winding stone stairs to the Norman Chapel where all admired it's stained glass windows then on they went down to the Undercroft.

'Very popular the Undie, packed out all year this is - not surprising being the student bar!'

On they went into the Great Hall.

'Very popular with the students this is. It's where they get their porridge after they've been out rowing on the Wear that early in the morning the mists have hardly lifted and they come in with fingers all frozen and blue on the nose.'

Up they went to the Tunstall Gallery.

'Very popular with the students this is. Study bedrooms as you've not seen the like along here. Some of them have arrow slits for windows. Not used so much for their original purpose of course these days.'

Along the Tunstall Gallery Aunt G noticed some portraits.

'Ah yes pet,' said Reynolds. 'All the important folk who helped build the castle throughout the ages starting of course with William the Conqueror. He set it all going with a little mound in 1072.'

'I say! Come and look at this Lizzy!' Aunt G was staring at a board at the far end of the gallery. On it were a number of photographs of young men and women.

'Isn't that Wickham, Lizzy?'

'You know young Mr Wickham?' asked the porter his tone changing. 'Of all the students I've known come through these mighty walls he is the most gormless gawk, rotten to the core, nowt good to be said of him. Expelled he was for deeds dark and dismal which I will not repeat in front of this delicate young lassie, mind. But what his picture is still doing on our College Board of Student Officers I do not know?'

And with that the porter ripped the photograph of Wickham off the board, tore it into little shreds, jumped up and down on it then kicked the little pieces into a mousehole that he had spotted between two large stones in the wall.

'Good for nothing little ...'

'Oh but Lizzy! Do you not know that gentleman too?' asked Aunt G interrupting Reynolds as she recognised the name of one of the other student officers.

'Fitzwilliam Darcy!' exclaimed Reynolds, immediately recovering his good humour. 'Now, hinny, there's a fine fellow. He was First Knight of the Castle last year, captain of rowing, rugby, wrestling, debating and jousting and the best young fellow anyone could wish to meet. Clivvor, chivalrous, fair, kind, compassionate, strong, brave, resilient, courageous, generous, wise, intelligent, bold, valiant, industrious ...'

'... and do you not think him very handsome too, Lizzy?' interjected Aunt G.

'Aye pet!' replied Reynolds on Lizzy's behalf. 'He is a most handsome young man. All the fresher maidens here are madly in love with him and I dare say some of the chaps too. Whoever captures his heart will be a lucky lassy indeed.'

Lizzy throughout was dumb struck. She had no idea that Darcy was at Durham, let alone University College. In all their conversations it had never arisen. She could never apply now. He would think she was chasing him! Oh the embarrassment! And the disappointment when she had quite lost her heart to the place.

'I think the young lady's besotted already!' teased Reynolds.

'No! No! You are much mistaken!' replied Lizzy, her emotions in turmoil. Then another thought struck her. 'When did you say the students returned?'

'Not for a week or so pet. And then all hell lets loose but until then the ghosts of the past have the castle all to themselves.'

Reynolds took them down the grand staircase and out into the central courtyard. It was a most sensational place. Lizzy, her mind awhirl with what she had seen and heard moved away from the group to gather her thoughts. As she wondered towards the portcullis she saw a mysterious tall, dark figure outlined against the sky walking directly towards her. When he was but twenty yards away the light shifted and she could make out his shape and his features at the same moment as he saw hers. Their eyes met instantly. Darcy! He stopped abruptly and stared, unable to move, momentarily transfixed in surprise. Was this an apparition? A ghost of the woman who had bewitched him and whose hold over his being he had so desperately tried to fight off. He trembled. Lizzy but ten paces away felt the cold hand of regret squeeze her heart. This was what she had spurned. She trembled.

A raven high up on the parapet swooped down, squawking, awakening Darcy from his momentary paralysis. He strode forward and grasped Lizzy's pale white hand in both of his. His eyes burned into hers.

'Miss Elizabeth Bennet! Welcome to Durham!'

'Darcy!' Lizzy could hardly breath. 'What are you?... Why are you? ... Where are you? ...'

Her words faded as they were uttered. She was enfeebled in his powerful presence. He towered over her, like the ancient turrets pushing to the sky behind. Her throat was constricted. Her breath came in short sharp bursts - yet through it all she became aware of a dampness. To her surprise she realised Darcy was wet through, his clothes stuck to his body like limpets, revealing his fine muscled torso as well as if he was completely naked. Lizzy was astounded and found herself unable to peel her eyes away.

'Oh my clothes,' said Darcy realising that the wet proximity of his body was alarming Lizzy. 'Yes, I am soaked through. Completely drenched! I returned to college early to train for the rowing season and have just met with a misadventure on the river.'

'I see,' said Lizzy in barely more than a whisper.

An awkward silence followed broken by Darcy speaking hurriedly, almost desperately as if he had made up his mind on some important matter and must get it off his chest.

'I have friends visiting the castle tomorrow. Mr Bingley and his sisters.'

Lizzy felt the awkwardness intensify and could only offer a slight gasp in response.

'And with them comes one I who would dearly like to make your acquaintance. My young sister, Georgiana.'

Lizzy's gasped again.

'Lizzy?' Aunt G's voice brought Lizzy back to her senses.

'This is Aunt G and Uncle G, Darcy,' exclaimed Lizzy as her uncle and aunt approached.

'Very pleased to make your acquaintance,' said Darcy nodding. He was unable to shake hands as he still had Lizzy's grasped in his and seemed unwilling or unable to let go.

'Do you enjoy rowing?' Darcy enquired of Uncle G, with the utmost civility and to Lizzy's great surprise. 'The college boat house is just down there,' he continued jerking his head in the direction of the said boat house. 'It is a beautiful walk down through the trees. The path is steep but I could lend you some stout shoes if you would do me the honour of joining me later?'

'That is most kind!' replied Uncle G delighted.

Darcy began to shake alarmingly. His hands were icy cold upon Lizzy's but he seemed not to notice. His face was deathly pale.

'You look cold sir,' said Aunt G kindly.

'Oh yes. So I am!' Darcy's teeth began to chatter alarmingly. 'I w ... w ...will g.. g... get ch..ch.. changed. Perhaps ... perhaps you w ... w.... will join us for t ... t ... tea?'

'How lovely,' Uncle G thanked him, 'but we have a

appointment to view the Cathedral.'

'O ... o ... of course! The c ... c... cathedral. Y ... y ... you must! A ... a ... masterpiece of the Romanesque ... don't miss the treasures of St ... Cuth ... Cuth ... Cuthbert ... or the m ... m ... monks dormitory.'

Darcy moved off, stiffly, but his hands were either frozen onto Lizzy's or he just could not let go. Luckily Aunt G always carried a flask of sweet hot tea in case of emergencies such as these, and holding it below the conjoined hands managed to warm them and prize them apart without as much as the smallest hint of chilblains. Freed, Darcy walked off as briskly as a frozen man can, bowing and waving as he went.

'Well!' exclaimed Aunt G after he had gone. 'What a charming young man Lizzy!'

'I forgot to say, pet,' interjected Reynolds who had been observing this exchange, 'that sometimes *some* students come back a little earlier than the *early* students. Such an example of this is young Mr Darcy as you have now seen for yourself.'

Chapter Forty Four

'I have a surprise for you,' said Uncle G triumphantly following their visit to the cathedral. 'Reynolds has kindly booked us into the Chaplain's Suite itself in the very heart of the castle!'

Lizzy flushed red. Not only was she imposing herself on Darcy's territory, she was practically staying in his room!

'Oh uncle!'

'I knew you'd be delighted!'

And that was that.

The following morning Lizzy, having risen late and still clad in her nightdress, was gazing at the romantic view of a medieval world through the arrow slit window of her bedroom when there was a knock on the massive oak door. Thinking it would be Aunt G, she opened the door and felt the blood drain from her face in shock. There stood Darcy! To think she stood before him so exposed! So revealed! The transparency of her garment! How it clung to her every outline! How the neckline was low, very low. Darcy took all this in, sighed wistfully and then announced,

'Miss Elizabeth Bennet! I am dry today and this is my sister Miss Georgiana Darcy.'

Georgiana appeared from behind Darcy, blushing and barely able to look directly at Lizzy. She was a handsome girl, her figure, though young, was womanly and graceful and Lizzy, despite her own confusion, warmed to her unassuming and gentle manners and felt compelled to invite brother and sister in. Hurriedly adding a matching silk negligee to her attire she offered them refreshments from the complimentary tea tray.

'Do sit down!' added Lizzy as she busied herself.

'Would you like tea or mead?' she asked reading the sachets on the tray.

The visitors opted for tea and Georgiana perched herself on a little stool. Darcy stood motionless and uncertain. The only other place to sit in the room, apart from Lizzy's unmade bed which was unthinkable, was a large chair hewn from an ancient oak.

'Oh Lord!' said Lizzy turning round holding two cups of tea and immediately seeing Darcy's dilemma. The chair was prettily adorned with her white lacy bra, knickers, suspender and stockings.

'Oh Lord!' repeated Lizzy.

'Shall I?' Darcy took the initiative and gently gathered up the underwear from the chair and placed the items slowly and reverently, on the bed. He then sat down on the chair and smiled at Lizzy.

'What a fine chair this is' he commented. 'Jolly good legs

'I am so pleased to make your acquaintance,' ventured Georgiana to Lizzy. 'My dear brother has told me so muc about you.'

'I fear what your brother might have said,' replied Lizzy warmly, 'but I am certainly glad to meet you.'

'My brother says you are a very spirited young lady. You must be to spend the night in this room alone. They say the castle is haunted. I would be frightened to death of ghosts and ghouls and would not sleep a wink!'

At that moment there was a curious moaning sound from behind the door.

'You see!' said Georgiana in horror. 'It *is* haunted!'

The ghostly moaning was heard again.

Georgiana leapt to Darcy, throwing her arms about him for protection and Lizzy herself felt a tinge of fear. The moaning grew louder.

'It might be the wife of one of the former Prince Bishops of Durham,' whispered Georgiana. 'I read about her last night. She haunts the black staircase; she fell down it and broke her neck!'

This time the moaning was accompanied by a faint clanking.

'Stay here!' said Darcy. 'Elizabeth, look after Georgiana and whatever you do don't come out. Whatever you hear, however fearful, stay right where you are. I'm going to see what it is. Georgiana, you will be safe with Elizabeth.'

Lizzy, though with a growing feeling of dread that the paranormal was upon them, nevertheless felt the compliment from Darcy. Their eyes met and lingered.

'Take care,' she whispered.

'I'll be back,' replied Darcy, echoing her whisper and he crossed the room, slowly opened the creaking door and was gone.

Lizzy and Georgiana took comfort by sitting together on the ancient chair, the younger girl holding tightly onto the older girls hands. They did not speak. They hardly dared to breath so desperate were they to hear what could be happening beyond the great oak door.

To begin with there was only deathly silence. Then there was a great clanking and somebody, not Darcy, said 'Gotcha!' and laughed in delight. It was a familiar laugh although Lizzy could not quite place it.

The door opened again. Darcy entered with a knight in armour following.

'Bingley!' said Darcy and sat down on the bed.

'Hello! Hello!' said Bingley springing open his visor. 'I hope I didn't frighten you. I was just so dying to try on one of these suits of armour that seemed to be scattered around all over the place in this ancient castle and then ... well one little thought led to another ... and I thought it would be quite a merry joke to spook you! Did I take you in? Did I?'

'You did, so we are doubly pleased to see you,' said Lizzy, her eyes shining in delight at being reunited with the young man.

Meanwhile, the commotion had brought the Gardiners, also still in a state of undress, rushing from their room. It was a curious meeting, half the people fully clothed, half still in nightwear and one in knight's armour but the atmosphere was jolly and good humour was apparent on both sides. On seeing Bingley, Lizzy's thoughts had immediately turned to Jane. Could it be that the young man retained any affection for her? Or had Cazza been right when she said Bingley was in love with Georgiana. From observation she saw no evidence of this. No secret looks, no paddlings of palms. Nothing. She found herself standing by the window with Bingley who ventured that it had been a long time since he had had the pleasure of seeing her. In fact the last time he had been with her family was 3.38pm Tuesday, 14th at Sunny Cove, just after he had rubbed some extra suncream on one of Lizzy's sisters' snowy white back which was beautifully decorated with a faint freckle two inches below the right shoulder blade and another to the left of her fourth vertebrae and just before he had left Salcombe for London. Lizzy was pleased with the precise nature of this observation and felt that there was still hope for Jane.

After further merry conversation the meeting drew to an end. Darcy had the pleasure of inviting the Gardiners and Lizzy to enjoy refreshments in the Great Hall that evening with themselves, Cazza, Lulu and Hattie who were expected to arrive during the day. All accepted gratefully and the visitors left.

It was only later, getting dressed that Lizzy was unable to locate one of her stockings. Fortunately she had a spare but she dreaded to think where the original might have gone. And it was only later that Darcy, on changing for rowing, found that the article had become attached somehow to the button on his back trouser pocket - probably when he had sat on it on the bed after discovering Bingley. It was too awkward to return and besides the sight of the item, it's silky touch and softness gave him more pleasure than he would like to admit.

Chapter Forty Five

DINNER in the Great Hall was an awkward affair. The ladies gathered first in the Tunstall Gallery. Cazza, Lulu and Hattie remained reserved and curt, Georgiana was so shy she spent the whole time hiding in the deep recess of an arrow window, peeping out, to view the company occasionally and retiring quickly if anyone caught sight of her. Reynolds brought a roast pig into the Great Hall and encouraged the ladies to tuck in before the gents arrived. The conversation had reached a low ebb and so whilst they seemed unable to speak, the ladies were able to eat. Lizzy was desperate for the gentlemen to appear. Half an hour later Darcy and Bingley stood before them. Cazza not yet beaten by Lizzy threw herself upon Darcy, encouraging him to sit by her and showing off her decolletage to its best effect, yet with little effect. This made her angry and she turned her jealous passion upon Lizzy.

'Eliza, are not the lifeguards now confined for their training at South Sands? How trying that must be for *your* family!'

Lifeguards instantly bought the name of Wickham to the minds of several in the room. The vicious dig intended for Lizzy also sent a knife into the heart of Darcy, and worse Georgiana, who still too shy to join them remained in the Tunstall Gallery but could hear every word. Still recovering from her near elopement she fell in a faint into the recess. After trifle Lizzy and the Gardiners left, and Cazza, Hattie and Lulu had an enjoyable time knocking back vodka and tonic whilst tearing Lizzy's character and looks apart.

'Totally sad, a complete waster' was Hattie's view

'Did you see her earrings? Costume jewellery,' chortled Lulu. 'So cheap!'

Cazza tried to draw Darcy in. 'Did you admire her earrings, Darcy? Do you think they set off her face to best advantage? I do recall you thought her rather pretty at one time?'

'I did once think her pretty. Now I consider her one of the handsomest women in my acquaintance,' retorted Darcy knocking back the tailend of a glass of single malt whiskey and retiring uneasily to bed.

Chapter Forty Six

THE following morning Lizzy had a text from Jane 'Hey Lizzie, Lydia run off with Wickham. Gone 2 Newquay Parentals crazy! Jane :('

A second text followed almost immediately:

'Lizzie, Lydia not just 2 Newquay. It's worse - much worse - mega worse. Yes she has gone 2 Newquay but no money s

Wickham has got Lydia job in a club. Not just bar work. Think poles (not country). Parentals freaking out in Salcombe! Come back urgently! Jane :-('

At that moment Darcy appeared at the door. Lizzy in her distress revealed the ghastly news.

'Newquay,' he muttered.

Lizzy through her tears went on to explain about Lydia's new career.

'Poles!' exclaimed Darcy and left.

'Oh foolish Lydia!' cried Lizzy bursting into tears and grabbing her Quba bag and accompanied by her uncle and her aunt, she caught the next train back to Salcombe.

Chapter Forty Seven

A sound of moaning reached Lizzy's ears before she reached 3 Island Street. The house was indeed in uproar!

Jane was waiting anxiously on the street for Lizzy's arrival. The girls embraced, with tears in their eyes and Jane between sobs gave Lizzy a crisis update.

Mr Bennet, who on hearing the dreadful news had set off immediately to trawl the lapdancing clubs of north Cornwall to try and recover his daughter. On hearing this, Uncle G bravely said he too would try and rescue his lost niece and he also set off, some observers noted, in particularly good spirits, for the lapdancing clubs of north Cornwall.

Meanwhile Kitty was constantly crying because *she* wanted to go to Newquay.

'It's so unfair. Lydia's clubbing and I'm crabbing.' Kitty just could not see the problem. 'I don't see what's wrong with Newquay. Just because it's common and everyone has raves on beaches and Lydia might be doing a bit of lapdancing - but I mean what's the difference wearing your bikini on the beach in the day or wearing your bikini in the evening and sliding down a pole?'

Mary wisely whispered to Lizzy,

'This is a most unfortunate affair; and will probably be much talked of. But we must stem the tide of malice, and pour into the wounded bosoms of each other the balm of sisterly consolation.'

Lizzy thanked her sister and promised to exchange balm as and when necessary then dashed upstairs to see her mother who was lying in bed moaning 'Newquay! Newquay! Of all the places in Britain this is the hardest to bear. My poor Lydia, dragged as a sex slave into a lapdancing club against her will by the villainous Wickham! Oh it's too much to bear'

Too much to bear it was indeed. As Lizzy picked up the pieces of what was becoming known throughout Salcombe as 'Polegate', it emerged Lydia, at the point of throwing reputation to the wind, had left a message. A text had been sent to Colonel Forster's wife.

'Escaped to Newquay at last with my Wicky! Deffo better than Salcombe! Wicky got me a gr8 job. Says just need my bikini. That's it! We'll get loadsa tips and share them 50:50. My darling Wicky is so kind and generous. How my sisters will be green with envy!! lol. Lydia :-)'

'Oh thoughtless, foolish Lydia!' cried Lizzy. All that could be hoped now was that Mr Bennet and Uncle G would be able to bring the headstrong girl back before the sins of Newquay took their toll.

Chapter Forty Eight

As news of Polegate spread Wickham's name became mud in Salcombe. It turned out he had debts in every pub, girls who had gone out with him for an innocent drink were under suspicion of having been seduced, and any young man who had gone out for a drink with him remembered Wickham only being on the receiving end of a round, never buying a round

Bad news was constantly followed by worse news. Wickham, it seemed had feigned an interest in diving. His true motive however had not been to admire the watery depths but to plunder the precious wrecks around the South Coast. Fortunately he had failed to find any treasure but he had gained another name. A rogue, a cheat and now a plunderer. Could his reputation sink any lower?

Mr Collins, enjoying the horror, sent an email to the Bennets to console, adding that 'the death of Lydia would have been a blessing in comparison'.

Meanwhile, Mr Bennet returned from Newquay having thoroughly investigated the lapdancing clubs, his hair wild and unkempt, his eyes rolling with a crazed look and a curiously happy smile on his lips, but with no Lydia.

Chapter Forty Nine

THE following day, under flat grey skies, Lizzy and Jane were plodding slowly through the mud flats of the outgoing tide with only three great cormorants and a little egret for company, when they had a text from their father. 'News!'

At once the girls dashed through the mud, sending the peaceful birds squawking to the skies in panic and splattering themselves from head to toe in their anxiety to hear what their father had to say. Mr Bennet was sitting on the thwart in Angelica which was aground, his mouth wide open and a puzzled look upon his face.

'Read it!' he said passing Lizzy the phone.

The text was from Uncle G.

'Found her!'

'Awesome!' exclaimed Jane in delight.

'Searched all nightclubs, pubs and exhausted myself in the myriad of lapdancing clubs. Tracked Lydia and Wickham down at club called 'Tottie's'. Lydia signed up for three year contract with severe penalties. By hook or by crook contract payed off and Lydia and Wickham bribed with allowance at Fat Face. Accepted with alacrity.'

'Oh splendid! Splendid!' cried Jane. 'But father, why do you look so crazed at this fine news?'

'What does he mean by 'by hook or by crook'? And as for an allowance at Fat Face? There must be at least White Stuff involved. And if so - how am I ever going to repay your uncle?'

Chapter Fifty

LYDIA it seemed was safe at last. She returned to 3 Island Street, apparently intact though with a tattoo of an anchor on the back of her neck and a sheepish Wickham in tow. She delighted in teasing her elder siblings that she now had a proper boyfriend and everything thereafter was 'My boyfriend this ...' and 'My boyfriend that ...' Wickham was welcomed with open arms into the bosom of Mrs Bennet who, on seeing Lydia, had recovered immediately. It seemed the lies and deceptions of Polegate were over.

Chapter Fifty One

'SO mother, what do you think of my *boyfriend*?' Lydia asked the delighted Mrs Bennet. 'Don't you wish your elder daughters were no longer on the shelf?'

This was too much for Lizzy and Jane, who rushed out in tears.

Later that day the girls were sitting on the quayside admiring Wickham's fine windsurfing talents - or at least Lydia was admiring him when she happened to say: 'Aren' things strange. Here I am with my *boyfriend* and you, Jane and Lizzy with none. But never mind. You never know what might turn up. Talking of turning up, wasn't it strange that that horrible Mr Darcy came into Tottie's with Uncle G and dragged me away - just as I was about to get my best tip ever! Can you believe it! Just as we were leaving the manager came out and Darcy had a real hoo hah with him and got me struck off my contract that dear Wickham had worked so hard to set up!' Lydia clasped her hand to her mouth. ' ... oh! - it was all meant to be a secret! Oh fish hooks!'

Lizzy nearly fell off the quayside in shock. So *Darcy* was the saviour! Oh lor! Darcy! Questions, rapid and wild, crowded her mind. Feelings, passions, possibilities rose to the surface and were then quelled immediately by reasoning. She walked on into town but nothing could distract her; not Jane imploring her to try on the bright pink sweatpants in Jack Wills that she had long coveted; not the glorious site of 'Bolt', 'Cadmus' and 'Wolf'; the rowing club's Cornish Pilot Gigs out training: not the site of a common heron standing on the shoreline; not the sudden dramatic exit of the The Baltic Exchange III all weather lifeboat, leaving it's pontooon on a rescue mission; not even Lydia offering to buy her a ginger and honeycomb ice cream from Salcombe Dairy. No! Her mind was in turmoil. Unable to relax in ignorance Lizzie determined to send a text to Aunt G begging her to clarify, to explain, to enable her to comprehend this extraordinary occurance.

Chapter Fifty Two

LIZZY's text, as she was scrambling about the rocks on Mill Bay later that day, from Aunt G was to surprise her further.

'My dear Lizzie'

Dear Aunt G. She always used text as if writing a letter.

'How strange! I thought you knew all otherwise Uncle G may not have acted as he did. But never mind that now. I will tell you what you are so anxious to hear.

When Lydia disappeared and Uncle G went to find her he was surprised to meet with Darcy in Newquay. Darcy it appeared had discovered Lydia and Wickham's whereabouts! I am sorry to say that Wickham has behaved most abominably and Lydia barely any better. Darcy apologised saying that he knew of the dangers of Wickham's character and felt it was almost his fault. Lydia should have been warned. Warned! I ask you. She, unlike you and Jane, is a silly goose and in my opinion has behaved very badly. I digress, however. Darcy with great generosity sorted out the contract. He did all this with'

Oh! Aunt G! With what? How frustrating! The text ended and nothing more was waiting. But Lizzy had learnt enough. It *was* Darcy. But why? Could he really have done such a thing because he felt responsible? A quiet voice she could not suppress murmured that perhaps he had done it all for *her*? She checked the thought. How ridiculous. She had rejected him once and besides, the last thing he would want would be to go out with a girl whose sister was going out with the abhorred Wickham. At that moment Wickham himself appeared from behind a large seaweed clad outcrop.

'Lizzy!' he said in surprise.

'Wickham!' she returned, challenging.

He grinned up at her, trying to gauge her feelings, but then slipped and looked likely to fall into the swirling sea below. Lizzy grasped him just in time and his fate hung with her. After a fleeting hesitation her kind heartedness and good sense won over. 'Come Wickham we are brother and sister now. Let us no longer argue,' and she pulled him back to safety, slapped him heartily on the back and linking his arm in hers they walked back along the sunlit beach.

Chapter Fifty Three

SOON after her Newquay adventures, Lydia awoke one morning having had a vivid dream that her life would change and she was destined to do great things. This played on her mind. Deep in thought she made a cup of coffee and went to sit on the bench outside the Over 60's Club, overlooking the harbour. A frail elderly lady with skin as delicate as parchment and hair so wispy it was hardly there seemed to appear from nowhere and perched on the bench besides Lydia. They fell into conversation. In a faint, whispery voice that at the same time had a mysterious strength and directness that pierced Lydia's very soul the lady spoke of her own vocation. She was a nun and had devoted her life to helping others: survivors of natural disasters; abandoned orphans; victims of war; sufferers from horrendous diseases; prisoners; prostitutes; the blind; the deaf; the dumb; the lost; the limbless - even the lapdancers. Lydia thought of her own selfish life, burst into tears, vowed to reform and perhaps if God would allow, eventually take orders. The nun comforted her and said salvation was open to all who opened their hearts and lives to salvation. She took Lydia's smooth, soft hand in her own feathery fingers and whispered that God would give her strength. Tears flowed down Lydia's cheeks. A haze blew in from over the sea enveloping the two women and when it was gone the elderly lady too had disappeared. Lydia knew now that the dream last night had not been merely a dream but a vision and that God had sent the nun to speak to her. Hope surged through her selfish veins. She ran home, crying out that she had seen the light, was spurning her foolish ways, was determined to devote the rest of her life to helping others and administered blessings to one and all. Mr Bennet was surprised. Kitty was open mouthed in shock. Lizzy, reading an article on 'Sisters of Mercy' in the Daily Telegraph said that might be the first step of her salvation. Lydia saw Lizzy reading that article at that very moment as a sign so clear and bright and shining that within half an hour she had booked herself an interview at the Sisters of Mercy recruiting office in London, which if successful, would see her sent off to build a school for abandoned children in Ecuador for the rest of the summer holidays.

'May the Lord bless you Lizzy,' cried Lydia in ecstasy.

At that moment Wickham appeared at the door.

'Ready for the beach?' he asked Lydia cheerfully.

'Not the beach you're thinking of! But if you think you can be saved pack a rucksack with your most basic belongings,' replied the transformed Lydia. 'I am off to Ecuador on the first step to salvation. Come along if you like - but don't expect any fun and games from me!' she added winking conspiritorially at her family.

'Actually Lydia,' replied Wickham blushing. 'There was something I was going to ... I think I ...'

Wickham's voice trailed off. To the Bennets' surprise Denny also appeared by the doorway, and stood besides Wickham.

'What Wickham is trying to say,' explained Denny 'what he was going to say on the beach but perhaps best be said now is ... well Lydia, Wickham has decided to stay With me.'

Denny put his arm protectively round Wickham's shoulder Wickham stared at the pavement, unable to meet Lydia's eyes

'On manoeuvres,' added Denny as if to explain.

'Of course,' said Lydia in a whisper. 'God bless you. Both.

Wickham just managed a smile and the two young men were gone.

'Well!' said Lydia trying to take it all in. 'Well!' she repeated recovering herself and re-gathering her thoughts 'I guess it's time for me to get going too!'

So with hugs, kisses and a profusion of blessings to her mother, father and sisters Lydia, her face aglow with The Good News left, her new life beckoning.

After the shock of Lydia's transformation a jubilant Mr Bennet took himself off to Captain Morgans' for a full slap up English breakfast of bacon, fried egg, black pudding, beans, sausages, mushrooms and hashbrowns followed by thick slabs of toast spread with thick dollops of butter and marmalade to celebrate the miracle of his youngest daughter's redemption.

Mrs Bennet retired to The Wardroom - only to hear gossip that had almost made her choke on a cappuccino once more. Mr Bingley was returning to Netherpollock!

Jane nearly chocked on her tutti frutti ice-cream when *she* heard the news but denied to observers she was at all affected by the rumour. Yet how could she be unaffected? All her hopes and dreams were tied up in that one name. Bingley! How she had fought them, subdued them, pretended to herself that they did not exist and now all those passions threatened to well up again. It was too much!

A knock on the open door of 3 Island Street early in the evening, however, challenged her strongest powers of composure. Bingley stood there resplendent in swimming trunks and towel in hand. The girls were out in the yard at the back, busy making friendship bracelets so Mrs Bennet welcomed Mr Bingley in. Bingley walked through the little house with a hop, skip and a jump and out into the yard. Jane did not dare raise her eyes. She firmly carried on plaiting yellow over cerise over emerald green until she became aware of blond hairs tickling her forehead.

'Jane,' said Bingley, leaning over, 'are you not going to say hello?'

'But of course,' said Jane adding her greeting and she looked up into the bluest, merriest eyes she had ever seen and hope welled up once more.

'Who are you making a friendship bracelet for?' enquired Bingley smiling. 'A friend or a lover?'

'I ... oh ... ,' Jane was pink with confusion. Who indeed was she making the bracelet for? 'Mary,' she said for safety. Bingley looked disappointed. 'But I could make one for you!'

she added hastily, sensing his disappointment. 'What are your favourite colours?'

Bingley took the opportunity to sit down besides Jane.

'Cornflower blue, like your eyes.'

'And like your cornflower blue eyes,' giggled Jane, surprised at her own bravery for making a remark of such a personal and intimate nature. But Bingley was clearly delighted at such progress.

'Pink like your lips,' he continued, 'and let me see gold like your hair would be just perfect, more than perfect.'

The young couple felt a shiver as their hands, selecting the coloured embroidery thread, touched.

There was a cough from the front door. The girls peered down the hallway. A figure, also in swimming trunks with a towel slung over broad shoulders was outlined in the front door frame. Darcy.

'Oh dear,' said Mrs Bennet in a tone quite different from that she had used to greet Bingley.

'It's that miserable, moody man who always looks as if he's swallowed a lump of granite,' said Kitty too loudly 'And he's got a horrible hairy chest. Like a gorilla!'

Lizzy who had taken such pleasure in observing Jane, was paralysed. Darcy was not invited in by Mrs Bennet and so his conversation, being conducted from a distance, was restricted although he did ask Lizzy if she had seen her uncle or aunt of late.

When the time came for the two gentlemen to leave Mrs Bennet took the opportunity to invite Bingley to join them for a picnic at Starehole Bay the following day.

'Wicked,' replied Bingley, which Mrs Bennet took as a 'yes'.

Chapter Fifty Four

It was a blustery day as the party set off for the little beach, a not inconsiderable walk along the Devonshire coastline. The path was uneven and rocky in places and Lizzy was happy to note Bingley grasping Jane's arm from time to time, to prevent himself from slipping. They passed Sharp Tor and crossing the stream made the descent down to Starehole Bay. Mrs Bennet was all shrieks and alarm as the shaley ground constantly threatened to slip from beneath her and in the end got the better of her and she tumbled the last forty feet taking with her Darcy who had surprised all by coming along too and had been leading the way, alone with his own thoughts. Lizzy was mortified to see her mother grasping at Darcy as she fell, pulling him with her down the remainder of the path onto the beach where Mrs Bennet fell in a heap. To his credit Darcy helped her to her feet and they brushed themselves down and waited for the remainder of the party to make a more genteel entrance onto the sandy shore.

The picnic was spread out and the girls wrapped themselves in towels, and shrieking, wriggling and hopping about on one leg and then another, changed into their bikinis. Bingley and Darcy coyly retired to the rocks for their changing room. When they emerged in swimming trunks the girls could not fail to be impressed. Bingley was slim and trim and Jane had eyes only for him. But as for Mr Darcy! Fit, muscular, glowing. A silent gasp uttered by the remaining group of women left them open mouthed as he approached across the sands. Only Mary was unable to restrain herself and to her embarrassment let out a squeak, quickly covering her mouth to prevent further eruptions and then burrowing into her bag for her physics text book 'Electric Surges' to divert her mind and recover her reputation. Kitty broke the ice and suggested a game of volleyball before lunch. Bingley and Darcy were selected to select teams. Lizzy was desperate to see if Bingley would chose Jane first, which he did. Jane went and stood by him, both only too aware of the proximity of their nearly naked bodies.

'Splendid!' cried Bingley. 'Now Darcy,' he enthused, desperately trying to divert his own attention from the attractions of Jane, 'your turn!'

Darcy stared at the three sisters before him. Three young women in swimwear. It was hard to think with his usual clarity. His eyes moved swiftly from Kitty to Mary to Lizzy where they stopped, taking her all in from head to toe to head where they locked with Lizzy's. After a full two minutes Lizzy felt impelled to turn away but Darcy still did not speak.

'Come now Darcy!' encouraged Bingley. 'I must have you choose. I hate to see you standing about in this stupid manner. The tide will have come up and drowned us all before we have had a chance to even throw the ball if you do not hurry.'

Darcy opened his mouth and still looking as if in a trance at Lizzy, so tempting, clad in so very little, said very slowly,

'Mary'.

Lizzy it must be said felt some disappointment but smiled gamely until she was the last left, unselected and in the event ended up on Bingley's team. This did give her the opportunity to observe Darcy at length, who was observing her rather than the ball and this, combined with Jane and Bingley both inclined to say 'After you' before hitting the ball, led to a poor standard of play. This however, could not keep the young people's spirits down and once the game was complete there was a general dash into the sea. Much splashing followed and Kitty dared them all to a swimming race to Bellhouse Rock and back. Lizzy found herself swimming besides Darcy and they had a few polite words about Durham until mountains of surf reduced conversation to small exclamations. They all reached Bellhouse Rock successfully and sat to get their breath until someone said 'Where's Mary?'

'Help! Help!' came a thin cry from the seas.

Mary was in the process of drowning. Bingley and Darcy

gamely dived in and hauled her out of the water and while Bingley pumped her chest it fell to Darcy, reluctantly some would say, to give her mouth to mouth resuscitation. Lizzy was ablaze with emotion as she watched. She almost felt it would have been worth nearly drowning herself for such salvation. But she had rejected him once. Who could possibly expect that a man such as Darcy would ever repeat his overtures? No. It was over. Silly girl.

Back on the beach the picnic was a great success. Everyone claimed marmite sandwiches had never tasted so good and the prawns only made one person ill. The party returned to Salcombe in high spirits, Jane especially walking on air.

Chapter Fifty Five

THE next day was the crab catching competition. The Bennet girls were all lined up happily on Victoria Quay dangling their lines into the salty waters hoping for a big catch. Mrs Bennet was in charge of the net and every time one of her daughters carefully pulled up a little fellow she was so ham fisted swinging the net about that she knocked the catch back into the water. It was a most frustrating business, especially as nearly everyone else along the quay kept calling out 'Caught another!' in a most irritating manner.

Mrs Bennet was on the verge of giving up when the most amazing sight caught her eye. Mr Bingley rowing towards them! He looked so very perky, and there was clearly a bottle of Veuve Clicquot in an ice-bucket and two glasses in a picnic basket in the boat and a jewellery box that most certainly was inscribed with 'Tiffany' on the lid that, with a mother's instinct she knew instantly something was up.

'My dear Jane! He is come! Make haste! Make haste!'

But within seconds Bingley was upon them.

'Oh Mr Bingley!' said Mrs Bennet feigning surprise. 'Are you partial to crabbing? Do step out of your boat and come and join us.'

'Splendid!' replied Bingley remaining in his boat and making no attempt to get out.

'Such a delightful sport don't you think Mr Bingley?'

'Yes. Absolutely splendid!'

Silence ensued. After a while Kitty said, 'Chas do you think you could go away. I think you're disturbing the crabs. I've not had one bite like since you appeared.'

'Kitty!' said Mrs Bennet outraged and winked at her ferociously.

'Why are you like winking at me mother?' asked Kitty.

'I am not winking at you! But now thinking about it, I have some business with you. Come with me.'

Mrs Bennet managed to remove Kitty to the bench where Mary was already perched reading 'Quantum Physics for Dummies' (the last two words carefully deleted) and Lizzy was forced to give up her crabbing spot by her mother returning and demanding that she had some business with her too. Apart from seventy three children under eight, forty nine yummy mummies, sixteen merchant bankers, nine ex-hedge fund managers, twelve ex-bankers, two barristers, twelve judges and eighty-one exhausted grandparents Bingley and Jane were left quite, quite alone.

'Jane!' began Bingley, standing up. 'I ... I ....'

The rowing boat wobbled dangerously.

'I ... I ...'

Jane could hardly breath in anticipation.

'I ... I ..., ' continued Bingley bobbing up and down '. cannot balance ...'

Bingley wobbled again and a gasp went up from th spectators and one judge even removed his wig ready to jum in to the rescue of a potentially drowning man but Bingle regained control of himself and the boat

' ... very well. But you would do me the greatest honour

At this point Bingley knelt in the boat on one knee ' and make me the most splendidly happiest man in the world if you would ma ...'

Bingley and the boat wobbled dangerously.

'... marry me?'

The crowd were now captivated and all eyes turned to Jane. Before she could speak Bingley went on.

'Dearest, darling, quite delightful Jane. Say yes! Oh please say yes! I have a ring!'

Bingley opened the Tiffany box. If the day had been sunny and bright before the dazzling light shining from the ring within drew a gasp from the crowd. Bingley reached up and taking Jane's hand slipped the ring on her finger. Bingley held the lovely, slim, white now bejewelled hand waiting for her answer. As the boat drifted away from shore. Bingley was left suspended for a moment, not on dry land, not in the boat, but somewhere hovering in between, just long enough to hear Jane reply,

'I will'

before he fell in ecstasy into the water.

He emerged to see the beautiful face of his dear Jane searching for him and he rose triumphant to place for the first time a kiss on those heavenly lips.

Clapping erupted from the crabbers, young and old, and there was not a dry eye on the quayside, half tears of emotion, half salty water from the giant splash Jane made as Bingley inadvertently pulled her in. But who cared when such happiness abounded? Who cared when two young people were caught in such a splendid, delightful, seaweedy entanglement of love?

Chapter Fifty Six

THE following day a tremendous drumming sound swept over Island Street. The Bennet girls rushed out to see what the commotion was. Hovering above was a black Sikorsky 76 helicopter which to the astonishment not only of the Bennet girls but of all those holiday makers idling in the street, seemed to be intent on descending.

There was a widening of the road at the town end of Island Street, a flattish area and it soon became apparent that this was the destination of the aircraft. People duly scattered and upon landing a door was flung open and to the utmost amazement of Lizzy out stepped Lady Catherine de Brrr. She immediately walked with an air more than usually ungracious and burst uninvited straight into the sitting room of 3 Island Street to the surprise of Mrs Bennet who had been sitting engrossed in 'Hello' magazine. The Bennet girls hurried in and a side whisper from Lizzy who the invader was and her mode of transport enlightened Mrs Bennet who was thereafter all graciousness. After all anyone who arrived by helicopter, even if they interrupted a good read, must be worthy of polite attention.

'This is your mother I suppose, Miss Elizabeth Bennet?' said Lady Catherine as way of introduction, 'and that is a sister?'

'Yes Lady Catherine,' replied Lizzy, still astonished by her presence.

'I see there is a brackish sort of backwater over there. Lady Catherine waved in the direction of Batson Creek. 'I would be grateful if you would accompany me on a short rowing trip Miss Elizabeth Bennet.'

Lizzy obeyed out of curiosity rather than anticipated pleasure. She got out two life jackets from the chest in the sitting room, took the oars from the wall and followed Lady Catherine who was already marching out of the house.

Lizzy untied Angelica and rowed Lady Catherine down the picturesque inlet towards Lower Batson. Lady Catherine immediately launched her attack.

'Miss Elizabeth Bennet! How dare you even consider being engaged to my nephew, Mr Darcy! How could you! You are quite outrageous! An upstart! Mr Darcy is engaged to *my* daughter!'

The helicopter had now taken off and was following Lady Catherine's moves. Her ladyship waved with dramatic effect up at the aircraft and Lizzy could just make out the pale face of Miss De Brrr peering out, terrified, from the sky above.

'If he is engaged to *your* daughter,' said Lizzy, puffing violently as she tried to balance the boat to prevent it being swamped by the waves caused by the downwind from the helicopter, 'you can hardly suspect that he could be engaged to *me*!'

'Insolent girl!' cried Lady Catherine standing up in fury. The sudden movement caused the boat to lurch dangerously and Lizzy was caught off guard and fell backwards, almost into the sea. Lady Catherine toppled forward and taking advantage of her new position leant forward further, digging her sharp red nails into poor Lizzy's neck to emphasise her next point.

'And do you promise *never* to be engaged to my nephew?'

'I will promise no such thing! But since you are intent on killing me why should you care?'

'Insolent, ungrateful girl!' yelled Lady Catherine now incandescent with rage. Lady Catherine's nails were formidable and were locked onto Lizzy's neck as their owner ranted and raged. Lizzy could feel the final breath being squeezed from her limp body. Somewhere in the haze of near death she saw Lady Catherine signal to the helicopter hovering above. A hook was lowered down and Lady Catherine attached it to her diamante belt. As Lizzy passed in and out of consciousness she was aware of Lady Catherine being lifted from her and swept up and away towards the hovering helicopter, still screaming 'insolent, ungrateful girl!' The pressure released from her throat Lizzy choked and coughed until coming round saw the helicopter disappearing towards Bolberry Down, Lady Catherine leaning from the open doorway shaking her fist and Miss De Brrr peeping out of a window. Lizzy recovered herself and rowed back to 3 Island Street hardly knowing what to think.

Chapter Fifty Seven

THE day after the extraordinary visit Mr Bennet received a text from Mr Collins that cheered him up no end.

'I say Lizzy' he called. 'I've just had a text from Mr Collins. It will amuse you! Ha! Ha! Ha! It says ... Ha! Ha! Ha! ... that you Lizzy ... *you* ... may be linked to ... Ha! Ha! ... Mr Darcy! *Mr Darcy!* That man who probably never looked at you in his life! Ha! Ha! ... and there is more ... dear Mr Collins expressly advises against it as Lady Catherine would be seriously displeased! Ha! Ha! Ha!'

Lizzy, would have much rather cried than laughed but did manage to add a 'Ha! Ha!' to keep up appearances.

Chapter Fifty Eight

BINGLEY and Darcy took it upon themselves to suggest a walk with the Bennet girls over to Bolt Head that afternoon Jane and Bingley walked ahead, hand in hand, then arm in arm, then arms around each other shoulders, then arms around each others waists and with eyes only for each other. Darcy Lizzy and Kitty formed an uncomfortable threesome behind until Kitty, bored, spotted some absolute machines playing volleyball as they passed South Sands and decided they woul make better company than a dull sister and the odious Darcy, so she left. Darcy and Lizzy, climbed the steep path to the cliff top alone. Darcy seemed most interested in the seagulls and failed to look once at Lizzy, but she, gathering boldness burst out 'Thank you so much for saving Lydia!'

'Lydia! That was meant to be a secret. I thought Mrs Gardiner could have been trusted.'

'Oh it was Lydia herself who blurted it all out. We are most grateful.'

They stood on the cliff top where a gun emplacement had previously bravely stood to protect Salcombe, surviving the war, but subsequently destroyed by deadly health and safety orders. Now Darcy took courage.

'Lizzy if you still cannot bear the sight of me speak now and I will never ...'

A gust of wind raced up across the cliff and swept Darcy off his feet. He stumbled and to Lizzy's horror disappeared backwards over the cliff top and out of sight.

'Darcy! Darcy!' she called frantically. Could it be that the joy she hardly dared to hope for had just been cruelly blown away? Was her chance of happiness lying dashed on the jagged rocks below? Or could he be lying injured in terrible pain? The idea of his perfect body mangled tore at Lizzy's heart.

'Darcy! Darcy!'

Her cries were caught and tossed around by the heartless wind.

'I was just trying to say,' Darcy went on from somewhere far below, 'if you cannot bear the sight of me I will never ask you out again and will never ohh! ... '

Above the deafening roar of the wind there was a louder roar of falling rocks. Darcy's voice went on but sounded further away than ever.

'... I will never ohh! ... mention the subject again.'

'Oh Darcy!' called Lizzy over the cliff top. Her relief that he was still alive gave her the courage to voice her true feelings. 'Far from not bearing the sight of you I could not bear not to have sight of you but I simply cannot see you at all at this very moment! Oh Darcy!'

'Did you say you could or could not bear the sight of me?'

'I said I could not bear not to have sight of you!'

The wind whistled and snatched at their words, whisking them away so comprehension was almost impossible. Darcy tried again.

'I say, do you think you could make yourself clear on this Elizabeth. Can you or can you not bear the sight of me? It is rather important to my next move.'

'I cannot bear not to have sight of you.'

'What was that?'

The wind still mocked at their words. Darcy hanging onto the rock face with sixty feet sheer drop below and a devil of a climb above was facing the dilemma of his lifetime. He loved Elizabeth more than life itself. That he would now admit to himself and if Elizabeth could bear the sight of him he would try and climb up. If she could *not* bear the sight of him he might as well fling himself off the cliff onto the rocks below He tried again.

'Elizabeth. Could you please try and speak more clearly Can you or can you not bear the sight of me?'

There was no distinguishable answer. Darcy was desperate. Then he had an idea. From his pocket he got out an old copy of 'Pride and Prejudice' by Jane Austen which he had intended to read should they stop on their walk and conversation dry up. Reluctantly he tore out the frontispiec and scribbled a note.

'Elizabeth. Can you or can you not bear the sight of me Yours F Darcy.

PS Please roll one stone down if your answer is no and tw stones down if it is yes.'

He then wrapped the note around a bit of rock that h burrowed out from the rockface with his bare hands and thre the little parcel successfully up and over the top of the cliff.

Darcy's heart was racing, his mind in turmoil as he waited in torment for an answer from the woman he was so deeply, violently in love with. He writhed in passionate agony but immediately saw the danger of any such movement as the ground threatened to fall away from below his feet sending him to certain death. What could he do? Very carefully, hardly moving, to take his mind off his predicament he opened Pride and Prejudice and started to read. Despite himself, he was immediately engaged and struck with how well the novel resonated with the modern reader.

Meanwhile the little note wrapped around the stone met it's mark almost too well. It smacked Lizzy in the middle of her forehead and knocked her clean out. She lay, unconscious, on the cliff top for a good half-hour before coming round whereupon she eagerly dropped two stones over the top. Darcy was not sure if one of the stones was or was not intended or had fallen by accident.

'Could you be more specific?' came another note.

Two large boulders came crashing down.

Darcy now on Chapter Fifty Eight of Pride and Prejudice felt a thrill of joy surge through his whole being. He tucked the book into his breast pocket and with trembling hands began the ascent of the cliff face. It was a superhuman effort and for years later walkers peering over the edge of the sheer drop would marvel at Darcy's survival. But Lizzy's response had inspired him, given him hope, courage, a fearlessness. He found every nook and cranny on the rock face that could be found, every little projection that could be held onto was grasped and despite the wind, wild and whipping around him, trying to peel him away, Darcy clambered on and upwards towards the object of his tempestuous affections.

At the top Lizzy was lying down, the long grass whipping her face, leaning forward over the cliff as far as she dared, waiting for him. Without hesitation she grabbed his strong, muscular arms as soon as they were in reach.

Still in danger, the feel of her fine white hands on his

straining arms was almost too much. He had only the frailest of toe holds and looking into her fine eyes set in that radiant face he just had to know his fate before he could make another move. Hardly daring to hear the answer he whispered, 'Tell me, face to face, Elizabeth are your feelings as they were when I last professed my love for you? If they are I will never raise the subject again.'

Lizzy felt the closeness of Darcy's handsome face, the dark hair just touching her smooth skin, his breath upon her cheek.

'They could not be more different,' she replied, her heart racing.

The feelings of happiness this response evoked in Darcy cannot be overestimated. He was a man violently in love and it gave him the herculean strength to pull himself up and over from the precipice of loneliness and desolation straight into the arms of the woman he so desperately, ardently adored. Together at last! How long they stayed enfolded in each others arms in the long soft grass, neither could remember. But what did it matter - they were two young lovers, entwined, hearts beating together, thrilled by the crash of waves below, warmed by the late summer sun above, and the knowledge that true love was theirs at last.

Chapter Fifty Nine

Mr Bennet was painting the windows of 3 Island Street a cornflower blue selected by Jane as she felt it reflected the colour of her dear Bingley's eyes when Darcy of all people came by and asked if he might have a word. On hearing this request from such a formidable young man Mr Bennet felt much surprised but obliged to obey. The house being busy with female activity, the two went over to a quiet spot on the quayside where they might have been observed in various attitudes of awkwardness and surprise concluding in happy agreement as hands were shaken.

'Lizzy! Lizzy!' Mr Bennet called on his return. 'Darcy astonishes me! You astonish me! I know you think him a proud, objectionable man whom you have always hated. But if you love him too then who am I to object to your going out with him? He scares the living day lights out of me but I suppose it is jolly decent of him to ask permission in this day and age. He is markedly old fashioned.'

'I do love him father!' said Lizzy smiling and crying all at once.

'Well that's a good thing because I am in no doubt about the violence of his affections! Here take this and go and buy yourself and your young man a bottle of Moet et Chandon. It's the least I can do!'

Mrs Bennet, who had been eavesdropping on the news rushed out of the house, screaming to tell anyone who would listen, always declaring how she had been most fond of Darcy darling!

Chapter Sixty

TEXTS of happiness flew in all directions. Texts of fury exploded from Lady Catherine. Mr Collins failed to know what to make of it all. Mary just got on with her physics.

Chapter Sixty One

THE summer holiday drew to a close. Lizzy was delighted to receive an offer from University College, Durham where she would be able to join Darcy. In normal circumstances Mr Bennet would not be keen on a daughter going to the same university as a boyfriend but Darcy was in his final year and deep down the contented father felt a most happy marriage was inevitable.

Jane and Bingley also found themselves travelling north. Jane was thrilled to be offered a place at York University to read History of Art. Bingley thought looking at glorious paintings with Jane seemed a jolly good way of spending the next three years and managed to squeeze in on clearing, mainly due to his delightful personality. As a consequence the four saw a great deal of each other over the following years.

Mr Bennet missed his elder two daughters sorely but got the train up on a regular basis and enjoyed staying in the Chaplain's Suite at University College and having breakfast with the genial and entertaining Chancellor when the latter was at home. Kitty improved, inspired by Lydia's transformation. Lydia text to announce that the school in Ecuador was nearly complete, the little children adorable and she had arranged to spend the next school holidays out there spreading The Good News. To her delight she had also received a text from Wickham saying he had reconsidered and wished to transform his life too and how should he take his first steps to salvation? Mary won everyone's admiration for the number of physics 'A' level retakes she managed to endure and Mrs Bennet happily gossiped with one and all and made a regular habit of showing off about her daughters to all her best friends.

As for the Gardiners, during term time they were always welcome in York and Durham, and Lizzy and Darcy ensured they spared time from their studies to enjoy a delightful row with them along the river that flowed majestically below the magnificent Durham castle.

During the holidays, of course, everyone convened back at Salcombe to take brisk cliff walks, frolic in the sea, build sandcastles and make fine catches at every delightful opportunity.

The End